WHITMAN'S CHOICE

JOHN R. PRICE

Publishing Coordinator – Sharon Kizziah-Holmes

Paperback-Press
an imprint of A & S Publishing
Paperback Press, LLC
Springfield, Missouri

ISBN -13: 978-1-964559-96-4 (Paperback)
ISBN – 13: 978-1-964559-97-1 (eBook)

DEDICATION

To Anna, my wife, who has been so loving and caring all these years—a true blessing from God. Thank you for helping me edit this book for publication.

To Elizabeth, my sister, who provided encouragement and her years of English literature and theatre.

To Joe and Patricia, my late parents who tirelessly tried to raise my sister and me to know the Lord.

To Ron and Lori, my in-laws, who also have prayed and helped provide encouragement and thought over these many months for me to produce this book.

To Ray, Alta, J.W., and Zola (my late grandparents) who influenced me and my family to respect and know the Lord.

To Brother Jim, Bonnie, Neal, Tommy, Don, and many others who helped me understand and continue to follow the Lord.

Finally, to CCB, VVB, KTC, and CNC for the inspiration of this story and…that God would truly be glorified!

Thank you to God for touching my heart to compose this story!

IMPORTANT QUOTES

"When television is good, nothing – not the theater, not the magazines or newspapers – nothing is better.
But when television is bad, nothing is worse. I invite each of you to sit down in front of your television set when your station goes on the air and stay there, for a day, without a book, without a magazine, without a newspaper, without a profit and loss sheet or a rating book to distract you. Keep your eyes glued to that set until the station signs off. I can assure you that what you will observe is a vast wasteland."
– Newton N. Minow, Federal Communications Commission Chair (United States), "Television and the Public Interest." Delivered 9 May 1961, National Association of Broadcasters, Washington, DC.

"I will set no worthless thing before my eyes; I hate the work of those who fall away; It shall not fasten its grip on me." – Psalms 101:3, NASB

"Finally, brethren, whatever is true, whatever is honorable, whatever is right, whatever is pure, whatever is lovely, whatever is of good repute, if there is any excellence and if anything worthy of praise, dwell on these things. The things you have learned and received and heard and seen in me, practice these things, and the God of peace will be with you."
– Philippians 4:8-9, NASB

1

INTRODUCTION

◆———————◆———————◆

A s I exited the garage to our backyard, my feelings surged. I grabbed a stick of firewood and flung it at our fence.

The small log caused a loud bang. A wood plank splintered. Our neighbor's dog barked and made a beeline to the new gap in the fence. "Oh great!" Fortunately, Celeste and the kids weren't at home to see this happen.

Shortly after, my neighbor, Charlie, poked his head over the fence.

"Howdy, neighbor!" he said in his Texas drawl. "Are ya doin' okay"?

"Rough day."

"The way you tossed that log, I'm glad Alamo wasn't near the fence." Charlie raised an eyebrow. "Golly, you busted that plank into kindlin'!"

"I'm sorry about the fence." I turned to the dog. "Alamo, I'm sorry that I startled you, too."

"Are ya in a heap'a trouble?" asked Charlie.

"No, I really don't want to talk about it right now. I'll pay to replace the plank."

"Mike, I've known you for a while now. I've never seen you act like this before. Are ya sure you'll be okay?"

"I'll be fine. I need to get inside and rest a bit before Celeste and the kids get back."

Charlie reassured, "You and Celeste, let us know if ya need anything. Wife and I are proud to have y'all as neighbors."

I thanked Charlie and made my way inside the house. Earlier that day, I had lunch with Jamie Caballero, my agent and longtime friend. Following our meeting, I had called the studio to cancel my afternoon recording sessions. I couldn't believe how much TV and entertainment had changed over the last thirty-five years. When I started acting, we had only three major networks and a few over-the-air channels.

I can't believe this happened. How could Celeste do this? My wife of over fifteen years and the mother of our three children...I hope the kids haven't learned about this yet. Why hasn't anyone said anything to me about it? A reason occurred to me.

Celeste and the kids had gone to town with my mom. I noticed all of the photos of Celeste and the kids. I thought about how I got here—how we got here. How Celeste came into my life. I entered our home office. Looked at more pictures. Saw my awards on a shelf. A couple of old TV Guides hung in frames. I turned on the TV and began flipping through the channels to see what was going on in the world.

What was considered entertainment had changed. We had the Internet, and anyone could become a star overnight. This was what happened to my family through beginnings in the industry, and the series of events that upended our reputations. The industry and fans were rocked by events involving my family. This is our story.

I'm Michael Whitman. During my early years, I grew up with my parents and sister in north Texas during the late 1970s and early 1980s. Our dad was an advertising executive with a Dallas agency; our mom was a junior high math teacher. Staci is my older sister, by four years. For the first few years, we were a typical family in Plano, Texas.

With Dad working in the agency, there were often calls for kids to be involved in various commercials. You couldn't have an effective commercial targeted to kids and families without actual kids in the shot. The client didn't want to hire voice actors and animators to do the commercials. Many companies wanted their actual product in the commercial, not some fake. Back in the 1980s, animation was very expensive.

One day at the agency, Staci visited Dad. One of the team asked if Staci would like to read for a commercial. By some miracle, she got the part. That was her first commercial. Staci began acting in commercials at age six. In one of Staci's commercials, they needed a little boy to sit with a "family" that was the central focus of a restaurant. At the age of two, I got my first television commercial part; mainly sitting next to the "mother" while enjoying a meal. I had no speaking parts. However, the "dad" and Staci had one line each.

For the next four years, Staci and I did commercials from the north Texas area. Some were local commercials, but we had a few national commercials that paid better. I would've enjoyed continuing to do commercials for the rest of my life, but our lives were changed by another chance encounter.

In 1986, a television production company—connected with one of the major Hollywood studios—visited the Dallas area looking for at least one girl to star in a new TV series pilot. A pilot is often a test show to give the network brass a chance to see a sample of a finished show. As with many pilots, many changes can happen between the pilot and the first episode of a series. Sometimes, the pilot is aired with the rest of the series as a first episode. Other times, the pilot is replaced by a new first episode. I also learned why the TV networks had so many TV movies back then. Many failed TV pilots were recycled into some of the "movies of the week" to recoup some of the investment.

The working title of the show was *"Goodwin Circle."* It was described as a typical family sitcom of the day. Staci auditioned for the daughter. She had that face of a pretty all-American girl. They also planned to have a mother, a father, and a son. While at the audition, they asked Staci about her background and family. When they learned about me and my acting experience, the audition coordinator asked if they could meet me. Fortunately, I was with Mom that day when we went to pick up Staci. The coordinator asked for Staci and I to return to the audition room. Unfortunately, they didn't have a script that included the son. Staci suggested we improvise a scene. The audition coordinator was really impressed that we could improvise.

The coordinator explained that Staci was auditioning for the part of Robin Goodwin, the daughter of the family. The son's name was David Goodwin, who would be nicknamed "Davey" on the show. Staci and I borrowed an idea from our real life for the fictional brother and sister. Since it was close to Christmas, we talked about visiting our grandparents in a few weeks and what we were anticipating for gifts. As we improvised, the coordinator watched. I don't know what it was about the audition. Something told me that this was special. I really looked up to my sister. With her being there, I felt safe. For her age, she'd really matured in her behavior. I guess all of the on-the-job training helped with that.

When we concluded the session, the coordinator told us it was very good. She made several notes, including our contact information. Another coordinator entered the room and took a photo of Staci, me, and one with us together. As we concluded, we were told we'd receive a call within a few weeks.

Later, I asked, "Staci, why did you pick a Christmas story idea?"

She looked thoughtful. "It's a time of the year I really love. We'll be celebrating it very soon."

I looked up at her. "Did you think it was strange when the lady asked us if we were Christians, since you picked Christmas?"

Staci answered, "I think she understood that many celebrate Christmas who are not Christians."

I said, "We always wondered why all those people go around talking about Santa Claus and Jesus at the same time."

Staci paused. "For those that don't believe in Jesus, we have other things to think about. We have family and friends. We're thankful for the opportunity to spend time together."

I vividly remember that conversation. I won't get into a long set of details what happened next. I can say that our audition made an impression. We received a call later to go to Los Angeles for a final round of auditions. Ours was very special because the LA audition coordinators had Staci and I do auditions separately, and then two auditions together. Albert Jacobs, the show's creator, thought our real-life brother-and-sister chemistry shined through the camera. A few months later, we were in Los Angeles preparing for the new TV series that would debut as a mid-season replacement in spring 1988. They shot at least five episodes in the fall of 1987, so those shows would make it to air in the spring. We had to reshoot the pilot because the original actor hired to be the dad didn't sit well with the test audiences. Terrence Forrester was hired to play Robert "Bobby" Goodwin, an attorney. Marian Deavers was hired to play Bobby's wife and our mom, Caroline Goodwin. Caroline was a stay-at-home mom when the show began. However, by the third season, her character would go on to work as an elementary school teacher during the rest of the series, while completing her school administration degree. In the last season, Caroline became the assistant principal at the fictional town's second elementary school.

They got a "green light" from the network for a full season to begin the fall of 1988. We had a very busy taping schedule. Outside of the show, we appeared in the typical teen magazines of the day, on talk shows, and at hundreds of personal appearances around Southern California and our native north Texas during season breaks. Some trips involved visiting local TV stations to help promote the show. One year, we were involved in a contest to send four lucky viewers to attend a taping of our show in Los Angeles and participate in a VIP time with the cast at Disneyland. That was a really fun time to meet fans and share some special memories with them. I had a feeling that much more was in store for Staci and me.

During the show's fourth season, Staci met a guy. He played one of the many boyfriends that Staci's character Robin had over the years. Unfortunately, I forgot his name. So many people passed through our show. She told me one day that this guy loaned her a book that might help. He revealed that he was a Christian. The book in question was a very popular Christian one, at the time. Staci told him that she wasn't a Christian. The guy was astonished to learn that she wasn't a Christian, being from Texas and a typical all-American girl. Staci was told that he had been in acting since he was a child. Over the years, the guy had seen good and bad happen to various child stars. Because Hollywood can be a very lonely place, he felt that he was lucky to learn about Jesus Christ. His older sister had derailed her career from a roller-coaster ride of alcohol and drugs. Her family tried to find ways to help her overcome the spiral. He'd gotten a copy of this book from another friend when visiting a local church ministry, while on a break for a TV movie in Southern California.

After reading the book, Staci felt a need to attend a local church with this guy. She had a slight crush on him. One Sunday, she attended a local nondenominational church in Southern California. Staci wanted me to read the book as well. She thought that I'd enjoy it, and it would give me some stuff to think about. By this time, I was approaching eleven years old; Staci turned fifteen that year, but she looked more like seventeen. I think her looks and acting made her seem more mature. Would a ten-year-old really understand this book? I was no ordinary kid. I had learned to read scripts carefully and quickly. Reading this book was a breeze. It was simple and well written. As I read, I wanted to research some of the Bible passages that the author cited within the book.

Although our family didn't go to church, our dad had attended church as a child. While the Scripture and dogma did not stick with him, he kept a lot of books. We had three Bibles. One was a Gideon Bible that he received one Christmas as a gift. Another was a Revised Standard Version he purchased while he was in the military. The third was a New American Standard Bible (NASB) that one of my uncles had given Mom for Christmas a few years ago. The NASB had sat on the shelf untouched since being placed there in 1981. I found a little dust on top of the pages. I decided to use this Bible as I compared what was being said. It took me a few minutes to figure out how the Bible was laid out.

I spent an hour or two every day for a couple of weeks during the summer holidays reading the Bible passages and comparing them with the book. Staci attended a month of church services. One evening at home, Staci and I were playing a board game. Over this game, Staci shared an idea with me.

Staci asked, "What did you think of that book I gave you?"

I looked up at her. "It's interesting. I'm not sure I understand all of it."

"It might make more sense if you decided to go to church with me."

I frowned. "You've been going to church with that guy for only a month. How could you possibly know much after going for a month?"

"They were talking about this idea of being 'left behind.'"

I said, "I think I read something about that in the book. I wasn't sure I knew what they were talking about."

"At church, they've been talking about The Book of Revelation. It's the last book of the Bible."

"I saw it. I've been using Mom's Bible to see if the author's any good. The guy warns that some people purposely twist Bible verses. Every time I see this guy quote the Bible, I'm reading the whole chapter to see if he does that."

Staci asked, "Have you looked at anything in Revelation?"

"Yeah. It's weird, hard to understand, all that talk about trumpets, bowls, and strange beasts. I've had to look through some of it. The imagery reminds me of some strange music videos I once saw on TV."

Staci shifted her body. "The pastor has been explaining it by chapter or parts-of-a-chapter the last few weeks. They've reached the part about how those who aren't believers by a certain unknown day will be left behind here on the earth. Those left will have to spend time here trying to make it through the next several years. If you're not a believer, or if you die, you'll be sent to Hell—an eternity of torment."

I frowned. "I read that. How do you feel about that?"

Staci looked uncomfortable. "I don't like it when they say that's where I'll go. If I die before that unknown day and I haven't accepted Christ as my Savior, I'll also go to Hell."

I said, "From what I read, Hell isn't a place you want to be if you have a choice. That choice is on whether you accept Christ or reject Christ. If you accept Christ, you need to ask Him to forgive your sins; but that seems too easy."

Staci agreed, "That's what they've been talking about at church."

I gave her a look. "So, you're saying you want me to go to church with you and this guy who you've been seeing?"

She made a face at me. "Not exactly."

"Oh?"

Staci said, "I was thinking of getting Mom and Dad to take us to church. I think they need to hear what's being shared."

I smiled. "You're suggesting this guy takes all of us to church with him in his car on Sunday morning?"

Staci swatted at me. "No, silly! I was thinking Mom and Dad could take us."

I smiled. "Are you sure you're not suggesting that Mom and Dad take me in their car, and you get to ride with 'Prince Charming'?"

She rolled her eyes. "You're silly! You're really silly!"

I said, "How is 'Prince Charming?' Has he kissed you yet?"

Staci scolded, "Really?"

I shrugged. "I don't know. I've heard crazier things happen in this town, even on a Sunday morning. Ya'know, it's Southern Cal."

All kidding aside, Staci was serious about us attending church. The Christian book had been that spark that led her to learn more. Later that evening when Mom and Dad were discussing the upcoming weekend, Staci recommended that instead of staying home, we go to church with her. At first,

Mom was unsure and somewhat afraid. Her last church experience wasn't a good one. That may have led to her discouraging us. Dad was accustomed to Sunday mornings doing other things or sleeping in. When they learned I wanted to go to church, too, Mom and Dad were more willing to go, since Staci had piqued my curiosity.

I know Mom felt nervous about going to church. Staci shared with her the Christian book that both of us had been reading. As she reviewed the material and her old Bible, many of the passages began flowing back into her mind. She shared with Staci why she had been so traumatized by church many years earlier. Staci and Mom didn't share the specifics with me. I figured out Mom's experience had been an attempted, guilt-ridden, forced "conversion" when she was a teenager, in rural southeast Oklahoma. As shared by the book's author, this type of experience could be considered a "false conversion." When she left home for college in the 1960s, Mom's bubble was burst by the times. The experience strained her family relationships.

Beginning the next Sunday morning, all four of us piled into the car to attend church. We drove to Spring Creek Community Bible Church. The church had a moderate-sized congregation. At that time, I believe they had 750 members. It was a fairly new church plant. We were pleasantly surprised that the pastor and associate pastor had trained at Spring Creek Community Bible Church, a nondenominational church, near our native city of Plano. The Southern California Spring Creek church began in the early 1980s with a small group of believers. The church gradually grew during the next decade. However, by the end of our ten-year television run, Spring Creek would undergo tremendous growth as more people moved into the area. I may be getting ahead of myself. It wasn't "church growth methods" that grew this church. It was the true preaching of the Word of God that led many to join and become saved within its walls.

As we approached the church, I could see its large steeple and bell tower. A large cross was atop the steeple. Anyone who was passing by would have no trouble realizing this as a church, a house of worship of the Lord. As we made our way inside, we saw many people. I was afraid that because Staci and I were celebrities, people would try asking for autographs. Staci said that most knew she had attended the last few Sundays. No one was making a scene about a famous person wanting to attend church. However, security was on hand to stop any paparazzi from causing trouble. Back then, Staci and I were still obscure to most paparazzi.

As we entered the front door, we saw many people who had just finished Sunday school. This was something that Staci hadn't tried yet because she was still attempting to understand all of this church stuff. As we made our way through the crowd, I heard a voice that sounded oddly familiar.

"Hello there!"

It was actor Terrence Forrester, our TV dad. We were very surprised to see him.

"I hope you're having a blessed day, welcome to Spring Creek!" said Terrence.

I looked aside at Staci. "You didn't mention that Terrence Forrester was attending here."

"I didn't know."

Terrence smiled. "I've been out of town the last few Sundays on business. I'm so glad to see that all of you chose to worship with us today."

Dad spoke up, "Staci's been telling us about what she's been learning at church these last four Sundays."

Terrence encouraged, "Well, I'm very glad to hear that. I hope that it's been helpful."

Mom joined the conversation. "We didn't know you're a Christian."

Terrence reassured, "I've been for many years. Hollywood can be a very difficult place for a believer. I've been very fortunate to find roles that didn't conflict with my Christian convictions."

I asked, "How long have you been a Christian?"

"I've been around church all of my life. I grew up in the faith when I was young. I'd been Southern Baptist in my home state of Virginia. As I moved across the country with various acting jobs, I carefully chose where I attended church. Six years ago, my wife and I were one of the first families to join Spring Creek. I became a believer about twenty-three years ago."

Terrence looked to be about forty to forty-five years of age. I guessed that he became a believer in his late teens or early twenties. I was later glad to find fellow Christians in the business. Over the following years, Terrence would become a valuable friend for us. When my family needed assistance understanding Scripture or our Christian walk, Terrence and his wife helped us grow.

Over the next few months, our family continued to attend church and eventually got involved in Sunday school. We met many people who had lived in the community for many years. The majority weren't in the entertainment industry. Most were your average Southern Californians, eking out a daily wage or yearly salary in various businesses. Many of the church kids attended either public or private school. Homeschooling was a relatively new idea at that time. Some were homeschooled, but not as many as in later years.

We discovered that some of our fellow actors from other shows and movies were members of this same church. Some were very well-known. Others were more of the background supporting actors. We even had various behind-the-scenes staffers, show runners, and crew members. Many would eventually call this church their home. Some were unable to attend every Sunday due to their work commitments. Some opted to attend the Saturday night service. We often heard that some folks were on the road for a few weeks each year. Many of them made it a point to attend church in the communities where they were working.

Eventually, many of these people would stream the live Sunday service or watch later through online streaming or download the weekly sermon podcasts. From the late '80s until the early 2000s, many church members relied on tape cassette recordings that they could receive on site or could purchase to be mailed.

Whichever way they chose, the Word of God was being preached at this church. It was sent around the world to those who had requested. At the time, I had this feeling that something good was going to happen. In the weeks and months to come, I would discover that "feeling" was the Holy Spirit nudging me. The Spirit had started to work on me through the reading of the Word. Our parents, Staci, and I soon learned that God had a purpose for our lives.

2

THE CONVERSION

♦───────♦───────♦

Our family grew further in our new-found faith after a year of attending Spring Creek Community Bible Church. Mom's fears were relieved as she heard the Word of God. The message wasn't all "Hell and Brimstone" or any other guilt-ridden message. The ministry team taught in an explanatory fashion—no "sugarcoating" and no "seeker-friendly" stuff. Solid teaching was the focus.

By the time our fifth season of *"Goodwin Circle"* began, Staci had her California driver's license. We were living more of our time in Southern California than in Texas. Dad transferred to the Southern California offices of the same ad agency, with a small job promotion. Mom earned her California teaching certification and found a part-time job teaching math at a local college. Staci and I would drive to the studio each day to work. Of course, we had on-site schooling. On some days, we would do our schoolwork when we didn't have scenes to shoot. Other days, we had lessons scheduled around our scenes. Mom and Dad emphasized a good education. After hearing Staci's story of one of her boyfriend's sisters getting into trouble, I knew I wanted to have a backup plan. Staci agreed. What do you do when the phone quits ringing?

Terrence Forrester explained his concerns as well. He didn't start acting until his twenties, so he didn't know what it was like to be in Hollywood as a kid. Terrence shared that his son Matt had been a teenage TV "heartthrob" in the mid-to-late 1970s. By the 1990s, his son was working outside of Hollywood, in a completely different job. Matt stayed away from addiction, despite all of the craziness of the 1970s. Staci and I had a chance to meet Matt a few times. He shared his Christian witness many times over the years.

One afternoon after Staci and I were done with our day at the studio, we headed home. On the way, Staci shared some of her thoughts with me.

"I know I keep asking you about this. Have you come to any decision yet?" she asked.

I was confused. "What do you mean?"

"Have you chosen to become a believer?"

"A believer? A believer of what?"

Staci swatted at me. "You silly. I'm talking about becoming a believer in Jesus Christ."

I shrugged. "I dunno."

"Have you accepted Him yet?"

"Not yet."

Staci asked, "Why?"

I shrugged. "I dunno."

"I'm feeling really inspired to do it."

"What's keeping you?"

Staci answered, "What's keeping *you* from accepting Him?"

I shrugged. "As I told you, I dunno."

Staci admitted, "I feel a little afraid of whether I can keep honoring Him?"

Puzzled, I asked, "Staci, what are you saying?"

Staci timidly responded, "I'm afraid I'll mess up."

I assured Staci, "If I understood everything right, it wouldn't be what you *do*. You can't use your faith in Christ as a reason to keep on sinning. If you make a mistake and you're honestly sorry, you can ask Him to forgive you. He knows."

Staci kept driving. We stopped at a drive-thru to get a small snack. The afternoon LA traffic was thick that day. Staci wanted to discuss more about her faith. You might think that we'd have had security back then. We did. Most folks weren't aware we did. We were watched closely. Our parents wanted us to have as normal a life as possible, without being tethered to a security detail or a chauffeured car. For security reasons, when we attended ordinary school, we didn't drive. When Staci stopped the car, she wanted to discuss more.

Staci asked, "I had a thought: We're driving to and from work each day. What if we'd had an accident? If we're not believers, what would happen?"

I answered as I looked up at her, "If we haven't accepted Christ?" I paused. "Eternal separation from God, and everyone else who we loved that actually believed."

"I've said that I don't want to go to Hell," replied Staci.

"Then, there's no other choice. Accepting Christ is the only way."

As I was eating my snack, I looked at my food and lifted my drink cup to see the Bible verse on the underside. As Staci was eating, she turned to look at me.

Staci asked, "Whatcha doing?"

"Looking to see what Bible verse is on the bottom of the cup."

"I didn't know this restaurant did that. I'll see what mine says. What does yours say?"

I looked at her with surprise. "John 3:16 *[NASB]*. *'For God so loved the world, that He gave His only begotten Son, that whoever believes in Him shall not perish, but have eternal life.'*"

She looked puzzled and astonished, and then she glanced at the bottom of her cup, her eyes darting. "Wow! You won't believe what mine says!"

I grinned. "I could. The same thing? John 3:16?"

Staci looked peeved. "You silly. It's a different verse."

I smiled. "Okay. What's your cup's verse?"

Staci looked down. "I shouldn't have smarted at you like that."

"I'm your little brother. Whatcha expect?" I said.

Staci grinned, "Romans 8:28 *[NASB]: 'And we know that God causes all things to work together for good to those who love God, to those who are called according to His purpose.'*"

We looked at each other. She seemed stunned.

I turned away. "Do you feel moved now?"

"Let's face it. We still have several minutes until we get home. I feel like the wait is over. I'm feeling that calling right here and now."

"For some reason, I agree."

"I don't want to force you to make a decision now if you aren't ready."

"Staci, I'm ready," I answered.

Her smile trembled. "What do we do?"

"I guess we pray, but I don't want to recite 'The Sinners Prayer.' That seems too canned. It has to be personal."

"I agree."

We both took sips of our drinks and set them down. Staci reached for my hand. This was one of those rare moments I let her. We bowed our heads.

Staci said, "I'll start. Let's pray."

I could feel Staci's hands shaking as though she was unsure she was doing the right thing. I was feeling weird. I wasn't sick. Instead, I felt butterflies and a spreading warmth.

She prayed, "Dear Lord, this has been a long time coming. You've made a difference in so many people. On this day, I ask Your Son, Jesus Christ, to come into my heart. I need a Savior. I can't do it alone. I've seen and read how many kid actors haven't put their trust in You. Jesus, I accept You as my Lord and personal Savior. Please forgive me of my sins. You died upon the cross and rose from the dead. You did this to save me. I haven't been honest. I haven't been good. Please show me Your Way. Let me follow You. May the Holy Spirit dwell in my heart...and bring the comfort, peace, and joy that only You can bring. I ask this in Your Holy Name."

When Staci finished, I could tell the shaking in her hands had subsided. I felt a slight warmth radiate from her fingers. Now, I was the one trembling. I felt like there was no turning back, like climbing to the top of a huge waterslide. I was sitting at the top waiting to plunge toward the pool at the end.

My prayer was like this. "Dear Lord, I'm a sinner. You're the only Way. Jesus, I need You. You're the only one who can save me from Hell. I ask You to come into my heart. I can't be good enough to save myself. I ask that You be with my sister Staci. May she continue to trust in You forever."

Staci responded, "Lord, please be with my brother Michael all of his days. May he also continue to trust in You forever."

We concluded, "In Jesus's Name we pray, Amen."

Suddenly, the warmth radiated through me. My stomach settled. My muscles quit shaking. My nervousness ceased. My mind settled. We opened our eyes, and we looked at each other. We both noticed a change. It wasn't a physical change. We changed spiritually that day. Staci seemed a little stunned. Our consciences were settled.

I asked, "Staci, you okay?"

"Yes."

"Something's different."

"Yep."

"Do you feel that warm feeling?"

"I think so," Staci answered.

"Do you think that's the Holy Spirit?" I asked.

"I think so."

Staci and I would later learn that our acceptance of Christ brought the Holy Spirit to enter us. It wasn't just a feeling; it was a change in our lives.[1]

I stretched. "Life won't be the same after this day. We need to talk to Mom and Dad."

"There's something we need to do next," said Staci.

"I think I know whatcha mean."

Staci said, "Let's get home."

When we got home, we told Mom and Dad what happened on the way. The security detail that had been following us told Mom and Dad that we had stopped for a snack on the way home and spent a few minutes away from the restaurant talking in the car. I hadn't noticed that while we were praying, one of the security personnel had walked up to our car to make sure that we were fine.

Dad felt moved to call Terrence Forrester and share with him what had happened on the way home. Dad told Terrence that the time had come for Mom and Dad to make their own commitments. If the kids were going to be believers, there was no reason for Mom and Dad not to as well. Dad asked Terrence if he and his wife would be available to come over to pray with us. Staci and I were overjoyed that they could. That evening in 1993 in our Southern California home, Terrence and his wife Margaret came over. Staci and I witnessed our folks become believers. Staci and I reaffirmed for our parents that we had made the conscious decision to accept Christ as our

---

[1] Ephesians 4:17-32, Ephesians 1:17-20, 1 Corinthians 2:6-16, John 14-16.

personal Savior. Not one moment of that evening was scripted.

After becoming Christians, life didn't feel the same. For others who were nonbelievers, some discovered that Staci and I weren't the same on the set. We weren't complaining anymore about who had more screen time, more lines, and other stuff—like some other actors might do.

During the fifth season of *"Goodwin Circle,"* Mom, Dad, Staci, and I decided that we would get baptized. Mom had been "christened" as a child. That wouldn't count because the situation wasn't her choice. Mom felt some hesitance being under the water. Terrence and the pastors assured her that the water wasn't deep, wasn't cold, and the time under the water wasn't very long—a mere few seconds.

One Sunday morning at church, all four of us were baptized. Terrence was present. He shared with the congregation how our parents had discussed our decision. Dad had requested Terrence to perform his baptism. Dad was under and up from the water in a few seconds. He in turn baptized Mom. Staci and I pointed at each other who should be next. I simply said that Staci should go next because she was responsible for helping me to accept Christ. Dad baptized Staci. Finally, my time came. I asked if both Dad and Terrence could hold me in the baptism. Dad repeated what he had asked Mom and Staci. I declared my answer "Yes!" Within a matter of seconds, I was under the water and out. The congregation clapped after each of us when we came up. Terrence said that it was the first time that he had seen a whole family get baptized on the same day at our church. It wouldn't be the last time.

We had received a green light from the network for a sixth season of *"Goodwin Circle."* By this point. I was almost thirteen years old. Staci was nearly seventeen. The storylines had been changing. Staci had really grown up on the show. The writers decided that Robin Goodwin was in her last year of high school. Davey Goodwin, my character, was entering junior high. The storylines got a little more mature, but not too much for a family audience.

For the first five years, the writing had been good, but the show was starting to show its age. Getting a five-year run on a network TV show back then could be tough. The ratings stayed strong because we were part of a Friday night block of shows the family audience really enjoyed. We were scheduled as the second show of the block of that prime family viewing time. On the week we cold-called our first reading of the script for the sixth season's fourth episode "Davey's Dilemma," Staci and I had to call into question what my character would be required to do in the episode.

We were sitting in a studio conference room reading the first draft of the script. Rarely does a script make it through the first draft. Rewrites are often done to correct mistakes and allow other shooting requirements. On this episode, we had a problem. I started reading the lines with one of our guest stars Jamie Caballero, who played Jesse Maddalena, one of our neighbor's kids. The scene's setting was at Jesse's home. On the same sound stage, the crew constructed a special house set with different furnishings. Here's what I remember from that day:

The scene began where Jamie and I entered the front door of Jesse's home. We had some small talk about school and girls, and then a serious matter developed.

Jamie asked, "Hey, Davey. Want a drink?"

The script called for Jamie—as Jesse—standing next to a locked liquor cabinet.

I responded, "Soda for me."

"I'm not talking about that kid's' stuff," answered Jamie, "You want rum added to it?"

"What?"

Jamie bragged, "We have rum and other stuff in my parent's' liquor cabinet."

As I read the script, I felt a little queasy about where this storyline was heading.

"I've never had rum. What's that?"

"It's alcohol."

"I'm not supposed to have alcohol," I answered. "Why are you asking me?"

"I've had other friends over. They've tried it," bragged Jamie.

"Like who?" I was doubtful.

Jamie continued Jesse's brag. "A bunch of the other kids. In fact, a few of them are coming over this afternoon. We're gonna party!"

"Are your folks gonna be home soon?"

"Nope. Pop's on a business trip for the next few days. Mom's at a business meeting. She won't be home for hours."

"That cabinet has a lock on it," I observed from the script notes.

"I found a way. My folks don't know I can get in it…"

Suddenly, Staci jumped up from her seat.

"Stop it! Stop it!" she yelled. "This is wrong!"

Everyone turned to look at her. Some of the adults looked shocked; others were rubbing their faces in disgust.

"I can't believe the direction this story is going!" she continued. "Davey is going to get drunk in this episode and then try to lie about it!"

"Staci, what's the problem? This isn't the first time Davey has had a lying situation," our director interjected.

I retorted, "This is really bad. Staci is right. I feel very uncomfortable with this storyline."

"Look, there's a reason we're doing this storyline. Albert Jacobs and the writers were looking for a story for Davey since he's reaching his teenage years…what coming-of-age storyline affects a lot of young teenagers today?"

"Not this teenager!" I exclaimed.

Terrence responded, "This story's a lead-in to an alcohol awareness campaign that the network is presenting."

Staci's face twisted as she began walking away from the table. "Terrence, how could you!"

"What'd I say?"

"You really want to encourage this type of storyline?!" yelled Staci as she approached the door.

"Not only does it bother Staci, but it also bothers me. I'm not going to be the first drunk teenager on a network television show!"

"Kid, you wouldn't be the first..." chimed our director.

"I find it morally wrong!" I exclaimed.

Our director answered, "Kids, it's just a story. Mike's not really going to drink any alcohol..."

"Not only is it wrong for his character to be getting drunk, but you are going to have him try to lie about it!" Staci paused at the doorway.

I turned to our director. "Is that what happens next? I didn't read that far."

Staci yelled, "Two pages later, you'll see that Davey gets into trouble. In his drunken stupor, he tries to lie to his dad about it."

I shook my head at the director. "That's too much! No way am I gonna do this! The writers have gone too far!"

"Get Albert on the phone," our director ordered one of the story editors. "We've got a problem."

Staci steamed, "I'm not going to do this episode either if you are going to do that to Mike's character!" With that, she threw the script to the floor and left.

I remember the story editor and director chasing after Staci and demanding she come back.

In six years, I'd never seen Staci flip out over a storyline. This was the first time I'd heard Albert Jacobs— the show's creator, and a co-executive producer—had attempted to substantially tarnish one of the characters. Staci ran to her dressing room and locked the door. I remember several of us running after her. She couldn't stand the idea that my character would be getting drunk and trying to lie about it. I'd never seen anything like it before. I felt an ache for her in my heart.

While chaos ensued outside Staci's dressing room, I walked into my dressing room. Terrence stood outside the door as I sat down.

"What happened to her, Mike?" said Terrence.

"I think she felt a little betrayed by what happened when you wanted to encourage the scene."

Terrence reassured, "Mike, it's not real. It's just an act. When they shoot the scene, you won't really be drinking alcohol. They often use fruit juice—like apple juice—so you don't get drunk." He paused. "Also, you're underage anyway."

I responded, "Oh?"

"I once played in an episode of 'Gunsmoke' several years back where I was in the saloon. My character got very drunk. We had to do many takes suggesting that I was drunk. It was all an act."

"What did the storyline call for your character to do? I don't remember seeing that episode."

Terrence continued, "It was in the last year... I don't remember the episode's name. My character was an outlaw that killed an innocent man."

"Oh? Was there anything special about the man that was killed?" I asked.

"He was married with a kid and another on the way."

"I'm sure it went over well at church when that episode aired," I retorted.

Terrence looked peeved, and I rolled my eyes.

I asked, "Bad jokes aside, what happened to your character?"

"Originally, Matt Dillon was supposed to capture me and bring me to justice."

"Were you a Christian then?"

"Yes, many in the public didn't know me well back then. I didn't talk a lot about my faith. I was more of a character actor in those days. A few friends at church tried to make jokes about Matt Dillon coming after me. Margaret got tired of some of the police officers and detectives making jokes out of it."

"You said originally Matt Dillon was supposed to bring your character to justice. Was there a rewrite?" I asked.

"Yes, what aired was my character getting into a shootout, when Matt Dillon and Festus found him."

"Why the rewrite?"

"I despised the character so much that I suggested the ending be a shootout."

"Why are you telling me this? Because your character in that western drank?"

Terrence replied, "Yes. I also wanted you to know that I later had the opportunity to share with my church why I made that request."

"Should I suggest that the writers kill off my character because Davey is so drunk out of his mind that he doesn't—"

Terrence retorted, "Michael! That's ridiculous!"

I continued, "C'mon! People who get drunk do dumb things. I refuse to do this scene for that reason. The drunkenness isn't the only reason. Davey has to lie about it."

"Do you recall that this isn't the first time that Davey has lied about something in the storyline? It adds conflict. Children are known to lie about things. It's a human element about growing up," Terrence responded.

"As a Christian, I have to accept doing this role this way?"

Terrence paused. "So that's it?"

"Terrence, I've changed. Staci has changed. We can't do it that way anymore."

"You don't have creative control. It isn't your show."

"Did you have creative control in your *'Gunsmoke'* contract?" I asked.

"No, but that was a different time…"

"Times may be different. No, *this* is different. I'm a kid. It's my body, voice, and partial likeness that's doing it."

Terrence began, "But your contract…

I interrupted, "Does your contract now have anything in it to keep them from doing what they've tried to do here?"

"Somewhat."

"Then, Staci and I need Mom and Dad to review our contracts."

Terrence shook his head. "My goodness! From the mouths of babes!"

"Psalm 8:2. I think," I quipped.

Terrence looked amazed. He seemed to realize why Staci and I were upset.

I asked, "What are we going to do now?"

"Knowing Albert Jacobs, he isn't going to budge on this one. I know that."

"Does he have the final say?"

Terrence answered, "At the show level? Yes, but he's not the absolute last person. I recall a former co-star in another series that refused a scene for religious reasons. The executive producer wouldn't agree to make a change."

Marian Deavers walked up beside Terrence and looked into the room. "Gentlemen, Staci isn't coming out of the dressing room. They're trying to see if they can get someone down here to pick the lock or open the door."

"Maybe I can talk with her. She isn't upset with me," I responded.

Marian looked amused. "I've heard child stars throw a temper tantrum over various things. This one is a first for me."

I looked at Marian.

"You're telling me my seventeen-year-old sister is a kid throwing a tantrum, and I'm only in junior high."

Marian answered, "I didn't mean it that way."

"This business makes us grow up too quick. It's upsetting to Staci to see this scene. We've been fortunate for six years this hasn't happened. I'll go see her."

Marian, Terrence, and I walked down the hallway to Staci's dressing room. Mom was outside the door with the other parents and staff.

"I'll see if I can get Staci to open the door. Could everyone please clear the doorway?" I turned to Terrence. "Don't leave. I still need to talk with you after this."

I began knocking on the door, then Albert Jacobs arrived. He wasn't happy.

Mr. Jacobs grunted at me, "Did you start this?"

I answered, "No, sir."

Mom started, "Mike didn't do anything..."

Marian explained, "Staci became upset. She read ahead in the script."

"Please let me see if I can talk with her," I begged.

"Could we have everyone clear the hallway?" asked Marian.

Mr. Jacobs exclaimed, "Everyone, let's break for lunch. We can try to sort out some of this later today. Tell security not to bother sending anyone down to open the door." Mr. Jacobs turned to me. "I hope you can talk some sense into your sister."

As the crowd dispersed, Mom and Terrence remained.

I knocked again on the door. "Staci, unlock the door. It's me."

The door opened.

"Hey, can we talk?" I asked.

Staci frowned. "Come in." She closed the door. "I don't want them coming in here right now." She dabbed her eyes and face with different tissues as we talked.

"If you didn't hear, they broke for lunch," as I sat down in a chair.

Staci walked over and sat facing the lighted mirror.

Staci moaned, "All of this attention...this weekly TV show..."

I joked, "And all of the perks."

"We can't go anywhere without those paparazzi showing up now," she complained.

I answered, "Tell me about it."

"Bodyguards having to accompany us to just about any public appearance now."

"I know," I consoled. "Everybody wants to know you. They want to be your friend. They think you are Robin Goodwin, and I'm Davey Goodwin."

"Mailbags of fan mail. Autographs and pictures to sign," said Staci.

"I guess that's the downside. My shopping mall appearance a couple years back outside of Denver was a real downer."

"Oh yeah, I remember. The crowd got so unruly and disorganized..."

I answered, "I remember when two police officers had to quickly carry me out of there out a back exit into the waiting limo. That was..."

"Six years is a long time for a TV show. We've not had a chance to be real kids," said Staci.

I said, "We weren't thinking about that six years ago."

"We also weren't Christians six years ago."

"Time passes."

Staci whined, "I'm about to finish high school this year. It won't be long before I need to make some decisions: if I should consider college, continue a career, or look for someone to settle down with."

"I still have a few years to go."

"If this show lasts another four years, you might be able to enjoy at least one normal year." Staci smiled.

"Let's change the topic," I said. "About the scene?"

Staci looked disappointed. "What about it?"

"I'm still opposed to it. I won't do it. I'd rather fight it or let them fire me."

Staci agreed, "Me, too!"

"That's maybe why they won't fire me or you: because they won't have a show. Terrence said that he thinks there is a way to stop them from taking advantage of us like that."

"Screen Actors Guild? Mike, they could try to replace you, me, or both of us. How can we fight this?"

"He didn't say. Whatever route we take, we need to act fast."

There was a knock at the door. I called out, "Who is it?"

"It's Terrence."

I responded, "Just a moment."

Terrence entered. "You know that they can get someone to unlock it."

"I heard Albert Jacobs call them off. He must've thought I'd talk some sense into Staci."

Staci grinned. "Mike says that you have some ideas of how to fight for us."

Terrence began, "I had a fellow co-star in a different series years ago who complained. He went over the executive producer's head. We'll have to make a few phone calls…"

We returned that afternoon, and we "held our noses" to the horrible storyline where Davey would get drunk, would get blamed wrongly for the ensuing mayhem at the neighbor's house, and would appear like a complete jerk. I wasn't going to let that storyline stand. Staci hated it as well. The writers knew better than to write this junk.

Terrence suggested we call several people. The Screen Actors Guild (SAG), our union, was one stop. Terrence even suggested we talk with the TV Programming and Scheduling Department of the network. After some research, we were able to contact Gerald "Jerry" Knobele, (no-BELL) the network's Vice President of Nighttime Programming. Terrence knew Jerry from a brief stint years ago at Desilu.

In our last five years on the network, Jerry Knobele became a strong ally for us and all of the network's family-oriented entertainment. Jerry had come from a Midwest family near Chicago with some connections to the Dallas-Fort Worth Metroplex. He worked his way up in the production side of the business. Terrence was able to get around the typical office phone tree to get an immediate call to Jerry.

When Terrence got Jerry on the phone later that evening, he explained what had happened in our first-run reading that afternoon. Jerry was willing to call us at home in a couple of days. He wanted to make sure that—as kids—we wouldn't suffer any backlash in front of or behind the camera.

When Jerry called us, he was very personable and kind. He had a fatherly sound to his voice. He was a family man. He and his wife had two grown kids, and even a few grandkids. His history with the network and other production companies in Los Angeles and Chicago had helped shape his career. His career goal was to bring quality programming to inform, educate, and entertain the masses. If a program didn't meet the "inform and educate" parameters, Jerry wouldn't consider airing it at all.

As we explained our situation, Jerry clarified that they were wanting an episode for an alcohol awareness campaign to discourage kids from the illegal use and abuse of alcoholic beverages. As we shared our concerns, Jerry realized that we weren't ordinary child actors.

"Mr. Knobele, we think this scene stinks, because it goes against our faith!" I said.

Mr. Knobele answered, "You realize that this isn't a religious show, and it's on a secular network? However, religious faiths can become an issue for actors if a part causes them to do something against their conscience and their belief system. What faith are you?"

I said, "Christian."

"Denomination?"

"Nondenominational," I said.

"Okay. I'm Episcopalian. I'm very understanding why you may have some objections to the storyline. As a Christian myself, I want you to know I completely understand what you want to do. I applaud you're willing to fight for the Faith. Please keep in mind that not everyone in Hollywood and elsewhere is as accepting. I may not always be here. If there is a change in the network management, I can't guarantee the next person will go to bat for you."

"We understand." Staci nodded.

"Did the writers ask you what you thought would be a better alternative to this first-draft storyline?" asked Mr. Knobele.

Staci answered, "If I were going to write a story about alcohol awareness, I'd rather promote the positive outlook of abstinence than with coping the negative effects of drunkenness."

I agreed, "I'd rather see Davey tell Jesse to 'forget it!' on the alcohol. Davey warns Jesse and leaves the house. When the party goes wrong, Davey can tell his dad that he tried to tell Jesse it was wrong getting into the liquor cabinet."

"That would be a better story," agreed Staci.

"Unfortunately, Jamie Caballero as Jesse is going to look like the bad guy," I said. "He's a really good guy in real life. I wish there were a way to give him a redeeming message."

Mr. Knobele thought for a moment. Then, he said, "There's a way that we could do this. After the show, we could have the three of you—Staci, you, and Jamie—tape a special network PSA [Public Service Announcement] to run at the end or after the show to tell the kids about the dangers. To help him have a redeeming quality, Jamie can say that in real life he wouldn't encourage the negative behavior and attitude that his character chose. You and Staci can be there to support Jamie in the message. We might also include Terrence Forrester and Marian Deavers at the beginning of the episode to warn viewers what would be shown on that episode. By having them do the warning, they could encourage parents to watch this serious-topic episode with their children. Parents could explain why we are being very serious about alcohol misuse, abuse, and illegal use by minors."

"I like that. Jamie might be ok with that," I said.

Staci answered, "I like your approach to inform and educate first. Mike and I would rather help other kids than hurt them."

"I don't want to gain a reputation of an on-screen juvenile delinquent," I admitted.

Mr. Knobele said, "I appreciate both of you standing your ground. Unfortunately, I got the impression that Albert was using Davey as a troubled kid when he started this show."

"That was the past and before I was a believer," I said.

"Mike, I noticed a difference last season in your acting," complimented Mr. Knobele. "You appeared much happier and willing to do your lines. You showed more emotion and seemed more alive. You weren't being so stiff. I've also heard that you and Staci have had fewer arguments and complaints about screen time or other petty things. However, this situation isn't a petty issue."

"Maybe becoming a believer helped make that change. I don't feel as tired and frustrated as I once did."

"Nor do I," said Staci. "Seems like the day goes quicker. I have more peace than before."

"I'm glad to know that," said Mr. Knobele. "I hope you stay true to the faith. We have a lot of current and former young performers that are in very bad shape. The same can also be said about some of your fellow youth throughout the country and the world today."

"We'll try to make a difference," I said. "Staci and I want to do that."

"Again, I appreciate that. I hope all goes well. I'll see if we can get this particular episode's storyline rewritten with some of the ideas we discussed. Hopefully, these changes will be good for all involved."

"Thank you, Mr. Knobele," chimed Staci and I.

"Thank you as well, I hope to meet you in person sometime. My grandkids really enjoy your show. God bless."

We thanked Mr. Knobele for the compliments from him and his family. We looked forward to seeing what changes could happen. Fortunately, Mr. Knobele stayed with the network through the final year of our series. He was a truly kind man. At a special network meeting, we were invited to promote our show for a seventh season. This also gave us a chance to meet with network affiliate personnel from around the country with Mr. Knobele. Our real families and our *Goodwin Circle* TV family also received this special opportunity. He was a kind man with a big Christian heart.

The episode was rewritten at Mr. Knobele's request with objections from series co-executive producer Albert Jacobs. However, the revised version of the "Davey's Dilemma" episode became a blessing for the series. It became one of the most memorable moments in 1990s sitcoms and family television. I remember taping the special PSA that aired at the end of the show with Staci and Jamie. It led to some special speaking engagements, awards, and other accolades—more than I can list or remember.

Mr. Knobele retired from the network in 1999. He was often called upon for his expertise from various news and talk shows into the 2000s to explain the major changes that were afflicting the entertainment industry at that time. In 2006, Jerry Knobele died from lung cancer at age eighty-two. He left a wonderful loving family and rich legacy to our world.

3

OPPORTUNITY LITERALLY KNOCKS

◆————————◆————————◆

The Northridge Earthquake caused some disruptions for our show. Early on the morning of Monday, January 17, 1994, we felt the shaking throughout the San Fernando Valley. I thought the real Big One had hit. Fortunately, our California home wasn't extensively damaged. We had a few drywall cracks in a few rooms. A neighbor had a chimney collapse. Utilities were disrupted in various parts of the LA Metro area. Of course, the focus was in Northridge and the close to sixty deaths that happened. We were safe, but getting to work to do our taping schedule was difficult for a few weeks. Because of the lost time, the production company and studio decided, with the network's approval, to reduce the number of produced episodes that season.

By 1995, we were into our eighth season. A new cast member, a young actress by the name of Celeste Hernandez, would soon make her debut. When I met her, she was only fourteen-years-old to my fifteen-years-old self. What a first meeting it was! Actually, we met at our first draft reading in the spring of 1995, before taping that memorable episode. Staci's character, Robin, had graduated high school and was attending an in-town college. Robin was also volunteering as an assistant scout leader and mentor to her previous troop of girls. I recall in the fourth episode that season, they had several girls guest-star in a scouting adventure with a bunch of funny moments. In that scout troop was a girl named Deborah Goldrich, known by her friends as Debbie. Celeste Hernandez portrayed Debbie.

Let me describe this scene if you haven't had the chance to see it. Davey received the honor of answering the front door where Debbie was selling scout cookies. I remember that on the first take, Davey was supposed to answer the front door. Debbie in her scouting uniform—while selling cookies—was supposed to greet Davey.

Terrence as Robert "Bobby" was seated in a living room chair near center stage. Marian Deavers as Caroline was near the kitchen table stage left. I was center stage standing behind the living room sofa. Staci as Robin was waiting at the top of the stairs. She was supposed to come down at some point to meet with Debbie.

When the doorbell rang, I told Dad I would get the door. I walked from center stage to the front door and wall stage right. I peeked through a curtain of the door's side windows. I announced that it was a Girl Scout and reached for the door. What happened?

On the first take as I was turning the doorknob, I realized that something felt strange about it. The knob slipped from the socket! I held the knob closer to my face and tried not to laugh at my predicament. When the audience saw my unexpected reaction, they roared with laughter. Celeste told me later she was wondering what all of the commotion was about. One of the crew decided to ring the doorbell again.

"Hold your horses!" I yelled. "We have a *door* problem!" Laughter continued.

I turned to Terrence with a grin. "Hey, Dad! Do you have a screwdriver I can borrow? The doorknob broke! The girl outside is wanting to come in!" More laughter followed.

The shot switched to Terrence sitting in the living room chair with his newspaper lowered and resting his head back, looking upward. He shook his head side to side, laughing with the audience and crew.

The shot returned to me. I turned my attention to the door and said, "Hey, Debbie! The door's unlocked, but it broke. Could you turn the knob on your side?"

The door opened revealing Debbie. I continued, "Thank you. You can *now* see…"

When Celeste saw the doorknob in my hand, she started laughing while having trouble reciting her lines. Again, the director didn't call cut because he knew I was trying to keep the scene going.

Celeste laughed. "My name is Debbie. I'm selling cookies."

"Cookies, huh?" I was going off script and hamming it up. I turned to Terrence. "Dad, do we want to buy some cookies?" The audience roared.

The shot changed back to Terrence who was still laughing in the easy chair and now trying to cover his "embarrassment" of the scene.

The shot changed to Celeste and me as I turned to Celeste. "I'm sorry, Debbie. Dad is busy laughing his rear end off from my misfortune." The audience continued their laughter as I shook the doorknob in my hand.

"There was something else I was supposed to do." Celeste struggled with laughter.

"Staci…uh I mean…" The audience laughed at my gaffe. "Uh…Robin… Robin's home." I turned around to the stairs. The scene changed to a wide shot of the room. "Robin, I think Debbie's here to see you."

Staci made her way down the stairs and tried to play a straight face. As she rounded the last step, I turned and tossed the broken doorknob to her and said, "Hey, Robin—

catch!" The knob bobbled and slipped through her hands and fell to the floor with a big clang. I walked back to the stairway, collapsing with laughter. Staci reached for the doorknob and picked it up. Celeste kept laughing as the audience roared.

Staci addressed Celeste, "Debbie, my brother doesn't know how to open doors...he just likes to break the knobs."

Everyone erupted with more laughter. The director finally yelled "Cut!"

The director knew that I was really good at improv when things became unpredictable. When things went wrong, I learned to milk every ounce of comedy from it, especially in the final years of the show. The director was willing to allow the scene to continue despite the hilarious outcome and wrecked storyline. It gave us and the studio audience something to laugh about, and plenty of footage for the yearly Christmas tape blooper reel for our show and the network. Fortunately, they had the foresight to not destroy the footage. It made it to the series DVD packages many years later. This first take made it to the blooper specials. Dick Clark had a field day showing it. I know this because I kept getting residual checks many years later, when some of those TV blooper specials would air on cable.

On the second take, we had to reshoot because a crew member was late ringing the doorbell and kept ringing it as I answered the door. What happened on the third take made it into the episode.

The scene started with me at my mark from center stage.

I began, "I'll get it!" I moved from center stage to the front door on stage right.

I peeked through the curtain of the left side window of the door. I said, "Looks like a girl in a uniform selling cookies."

I opened the door. "Hello." Debbie was there.

"Hi, I'm Debbie. I'm selling cookies to raise money."

"I see. You must be in Robin Goodwin's troop—Troop 23."

"How do you know Robin?"

"Because I'm her brother, Davey." I said, "Would you like to come in? Robin's home."

"Sure."

Celeste entered the living room, and I closed the door. I turned and followed Celeste toward the living room. As we passed the stairs, Staci, as Robin, was making her way down.

"Oh, speaking of Robin, there she is."

Celeste turned around to see Staci.

That first meeting became a cherished memory. Although I eventually married Celeste, sometime after *Goodwin Circle* ended its first-run production, it was hinted in the ninth or tenth season that Debbie and Davey would become a couple on the show.

We reached our tenth season in 1997. The network was really happy to have us. It was a big milestone. Staci and I had practically grown up on the show. I was seventeen. Celeste was sixteen. Staci was twenty-one. The storylines were getting tired. With us getting older, we felt that we needed to end the show on top. We taped our final episode in the spring of 1998. I know many at the network and many of our fans felt sad that an era had come to a close. Our show received a wonderful send-off. Many celebrity fans stopped by the set to offer their accolades and adorations. Ten seasons is a long time for a television program and especially for a family-situation comedy.

Staci and I welcomed the change. We had no idea if we'd ever have as good a run. The show opened more doors behind-the-scenes. The pay wasn't bad either. Mom and Dad made sure that we didn't get big egos during the show or make large demands. Our final curtain call was taped before the studio audience as the closing credits displayed to the home audience on that final episode. It was—and still is—very rare that a TV show gets a send-off quite like this one. As our real names and character names were announced one at a time, the audience cheered. It was a bittersweet moment. We were ready to give it a rest. For the first time in ten years, Staci and I weren't driving to the studio to tape another episode of *"Goodwin Circle."* After the show ended, *"Goodwin Circle"* continued to garner interest among its diehard fans.

"Goodwin Circle" had entered its first four seasons into broadcast syndication by the end of our network run. Many local TV stations and cable channels were scheduling the reruns for weekday after-school entertainment. The residual checks continued to come. Like some of the classic sitcoms that had been syndicated and rerun before, *"Goodwin Circle"* had become a late 1980s-1990s sitcom classic. In 2002, our original network commissioned two network TV movie reunions. The first aired in 2003. This two-hour TV movie revealed what happened to our TV family. Celeste and I got married in 2000. Staci married her boyfriend Kyle Carella in 1999, that she had been dating since 1994. She had met him outside of the show. He was a good sport to fill the role of Robin's husband Bryan Brandenburg for the TV movies. Of course, Celeste and I portrayed our beloved characters as a married couple as well.

After our second TV reunion movie in 2004, we were ready to do something new. Staci took a break from acting. She and Kyle moved away from California to get away from the business. They welcomed two children to the world in the following years.

I had tried to read for a few acting parts. I was finding that the projects' quality and questionable content were becoming a problem. I didn't like cussing on TV; especially the issue of taking the Lord's name in vain. I didn't see a distinction between reality and acting if an actor had to do that. I knew a few in the business that took roles because they needed the money and held their nose playing some questionable parts. I later learned some were upset after some of those jobs. Staci and I were lucky. We knew very clearly what roles we would take and which ones we wouldn't.

In 2006, Celeste and I decided to move back to my native Plano, Texas. We welcomed our three kids over the next few years. While in California, I had started to do voice-over commercial work. However, technology had improved where I didn't have to record in a professional studio in Los Angeles to do the work. Moving back to Texas was a great way to get our kids away from showbiz. I saw the changes coming in the early 2000s. I didn't like what I saw. Celeste and I wanted our kids to try a normal life instead. If the opportunity availed one of our kids to do commercials or acting, we could be selective. Mom and Dad moved back to Texas as well, in nearby Frisco. Mom had retired early from teaching near the end of *"Goodwin Circle."* Dad was getting older and wanting to do less grunt work in the advertising office in Southern California.

Staci and her family moved to southern Florida to enjoy the year-round great weather. Kyle, her husband, took a job in the Fort Lauderdale area. I was glad Staci and her family moved to Florida because it was an easier commute than California. She did a few voice-over commercials for various regional and national companies during those years, from Miami.

Eventually, Staci started acting again in the late 2000s. They were usually bit parts, TV cable movies, and some voice work as well. We both started some motivational speaking events, especially when some churches had learned about our faith journey and where we were by then. Staci was more interested in positive, family-friendly fare. She refused to do anything that would compromise her faith. I felt the same way. Too many of the scripts that I saw in the late 1990s were very different from what Staci and I saw growing up.

I could've quit working and used the investments that our parents had made for us, and the opportunities that it could've afforded me. I didn't want to sit idle around the house. I wanted to have a purpose in my life. Celeste and I found time to help our church and a couple of parachurch organizations. Several private religious colleges and universities were asking both of us to visit and share our testimony at various times. It gave Staci, Celeste, and I a platform to share our worldviews to help make a difference for the next generation. All seemed to be good. Then, we received a call in 2014 that really surprised all of us. We had no idea how life-changing or life-impacting this next chapter would affect our families. All that I can say is that it looked like a good idea. This next chapter began a strange and unusual three years for us.

4

THE AWAITED RETURN AND THE
UNEXPECTED DECEPTION

——◆———◆———◆——

In 2014 Celeste, Staci, and I received a call from Hollywood to see if we were interested in an updated revival and sequel to *"Goodwin Circle."* I was unsure if a revival would work. By this time, television was no longer over-the-air and a few cable channels—if someone was fortunate to have cable back in the mid-1980s. The digital TV revolution in the late 2000s finally changed the number of over-the-air channels from a few to several dozen in many cities.

Albert Jacobs was shopping around a new and updated version of the show. I was told the show would be called *"Goodwin Circles Around Again,"* a slight play-on-words of the original title. Staci, Celeste, and I were all called to see if we would be willing to come back and reprise our roles as adults. Terrence and Marian were also called to make their return. Plans were scheduled for taping to begin in spring or early summer 2015 with the eventual debut in fall 2015. No network had been named in the initial press releases, but we were later told the streaming service, FibreTainment, was finalizing the deal with SYZ Studios to help finance the show.

As 2015 began, my motivational speaker role had seen an increase in work and clientele. I foresaw that the demand in the speaking field was a better option than appearing on a weekly TV show. I told Celeste and Staci that my schedule wouldn't allow me to appear during the first season. I was grateful that Albert wanted me to appear. I just couldn't see being a regular. Staci and Celeste were very uncertain if they could do the show without me. I told them that they would be fine. By late 2014 and early 2015, Staci and Celeste were doing a few interviews to say that the new show *"Goodwin Circles Around Again"* was in the works. By March 2015, a deal was struck with the FibreTainment streaming service to carry the new show with an up-front two-season commitment. Instead of a weekly broadcast, the entire first season would be available on the first day of the "season" in fall 2015. Binge-watching had become a new concept in television entertainment.

In May 2015, the pilot script for *"Goodwin Circles Around Again"* arrived in the mail for Celeste to begin reading. The first run-through would be in June, and the pilot episode would be taped. Celeste and Staci arranged for a condo in Hollywood, not too far from the studio. Kyle stayed in Florida with his job and their kids. However, they would visit Staci in Hollywood regularly. His job allowed him to telecommute and work through his company's Southern California offices. For Celeste, our kids and I would travel to Hollywood to see her.

As the first season taping was drawing to a close, Staci and Kyle made their plans to move back to California, as more acting jobs were becoming available. Celeste would come home on breaks. During the taping season, she would stay in Staci and Kyle's guesthouse, after Staci and Kyle bought their new home. There were a few weekends and holidays that the kids and I would fly out to California, when we could.

Let me backtrack to Celeste receiving the pilot script. As I explained before, a pilot is often a test run-through of a sample story to give the network executives and preview audiences the premise of the show. Sometimes, the pilot will be aired as a first episode. Sometimes, the pilot could be a TV movie that introduces the characters and a story. Since FibreTainment was bankrolling the show, the commitment was to do a half-hour situation comedy. I remember that day when I found the script package in our mail.

"Celeste, I think the script arrived." I brandished the mail as I entered the living room of our Plano home.

Celeste asked, "How do you know?"

"It feels like it. The envelope has the studio's return address."

Sitting on the sofa, Celeste asked, "Are you going to open it?"

As I sat down with her, I said, "I wasn't sure that you wanted me looking."

"I wouldn't mind. It's only the pilot," said Celeste.

"True," I said, "however, I usually like to be surprised what the episodes contain. If I read the script, that would ruin the experience."

"That's why I asked if you wanted me to open it or not."

I thought for a moment. Celeste was preoccupied with organizing and paying bills. I decided to read the pilot script. The pilot episode presented Robin Goodwin as married. What was strange was the name of her on-screen husband had changed from the TV movies. Debbie, Celeste's character, would make some appearances in the show. Debbie lived with David "Davey" Goodwin in their own home. Robert and Caroline Goodwin—who were the original parents—also lived in the same town. Their parts were more guest-starring roles when their characters were needed. My character, Davey, would be on a business trip or away from the house. Phone calls, written letters, e-mails, text messages, and previous messages left by Davey before the start of the episode would explain his absence. Davey was still alive and around.

The pilot script introduced four new kids. Debbie and Davey have one son. Robin and her husband have one son and two daughters. All of the original characters have aged nearly twelve years since the second TV movie in 2004. I thumbed through the script and saw that it was a fairly good first effort. Two of the kids were at least six-to-eight years of age. Robin's oldest child—the son—was described at least ten years old. I'm not sure how because the second TV movie didn't have Robin expecting a child.

"What do ya think of the script?" she asked.

"It's a little long. I guess they will see what will work when you get to the script run-through in a few weeks."

"What do ya think of the story?"

"Hmmm… It's a fair 'catching-up-with-everyone' storyline," I commented. "It isn't the most interesting story. Robin's husband doesn't appear to be the same person that Kyle played. I find that clashing with the old show."

"There could always be some last-minute corrections," replied Celeste. "I hope we can recapture the magic of the original show."

"It'll be nice to see all of you reprise your roles. Terrence would play a wonderful grandfather figure because he has grandkids of his own. Marian has two grandkids from what I've been told. They're her pride and joy."

"I wonder how often Terrence and Marian will be seen on the show."

"They may be on the set only a few days depending on the storyline, since they aren't the focus of this series."

"When I get to see them, I'll make sure to tell them that you were sharing with me some good memories and a quick 'Hello.'"

"They really felt like a second Mom and Dad to Staci and me on the old show," I said. "Now, you'll get to start with them on this new series from the beginning. I'm hoping some good memories will happen."

"How's your work schedule?" asked Celeste.

"I have a talk on Monday in Richardson. A couple of voice-over sessions on Tuesday. In a couple of weeks, it's going to be back-to-back voice-over sessions. However, I plan to see you off to the airport when you fly to LA for the rehearsals and tapings."

"As you've said before, you don't want to know the plotlines. Are you sure?"

"I've always been that way with movies and TV shows," I assured Celeste. "It's hard for me to watch the shows I've starred on before I know the ending."

"How did you keep from compromising if you didn't know the ending?"

"After that one bout with Albert Jacobs, I always had various stipulations up front when I would audition. Word also got around town what I wouldn't do."

"If that's how you want it, I won't share any plotlines until the show debuts," said Celeste.

"Just let me watch the shows. I'd rather be surprised than know. Besides, I know you and Staci will make the right choices. Y'all won't let the crew and the writers force you into doing anything inappropriate."

"Many crew and writers are coming back for this series."

"Keep in mind. This is the sequel to the family-friendly hit 'Goodwin Circle!'"

A few weeks later, Celeste and Staci flew to LA to begin production. Staci and Celeste arranged for our families to Skype and e-mail each other. Over the next few weeks, Celeste and Staci would let us know that the show's taping schedule was taking off. Celeste hinted that they had a small problem with the first pilot. There was a special reshoot with a revised script. The production team had stated to all involved to not reveal any plotlines prior to the fall debut. They wanted the audience anticipation to build over the upcoming months. Fans had been waiting nearly ten years since the last movie to see what happened to their favorite characters.

Throughout the next several weeks with anticipation of the fall debut, I saw various ads for *"Goodwin Circles Around Again."* Celeste and Staci made a few promotional visits to different talk shows. They didn't let on much about the storylines or any big changes. However, I noticed one day on one show, Celeste looked a little scattered. I don't know if she had a difficult day that week on the set, or if something was bothering her. I texted her if everything was okay. She said it had been a rough week, but she didn't say much more. She said one taping led to closing the set for the remainder of the episodes because security and police had to clear a fight in the studio audience. Family members weren't allowed to attend the tapings.

I missed Celeste very much during that summer. There were a few times that I flew out to LA by myself to see her. She stayed true to her word to not reveal any storylines or spoilers. I also did a few motivational talks while in California and the West Coast, so I couldn't attend any of the tapings. As the anticipation was building for the September debut, a few entertainment news stories had floated there had been some unspecified tensions on the set. Three weeks away from the debut, a news story broke. Season one would be delayed to January 2016. Celeste texted that there had been some additional issues on the set, but she wasn't allowed to text the information or really talk about it. She mentioned that they had already begun on the second season. They would be taping those on a very busy schedule. However, all of our immediate families flew out to California for the Christmas holidays. Celeste, our kids, and I were able to stay in the condo while Staci's family moved into their new California home. Staci commented that she didn't like having to move again.

During the Christmas holidays, Celeste and I were able to spend some quality time. Staci and her family were also looking forward to the New Year. They were getting their new California home ready for the holidays. FibreTainment announced that the first season of *"Goodwin Circles Around Again"* would debut on Monday, January 18, 2016, at 12:01 a.m. Eastern Standard Time. The second season wouldn't be available until sometime later in 2016 or early 2017. The timing was very unfortunate that we wouldn't see any of the new episodes until after the holidays.

During one of our family gatherings, Kyle thought it would be fun to retrieve their *"Goodwin Circle"* DVD boxset. Kyle was like me; he enjoyed watching all of the bloopers— especially those with Staci. With so many outtakes and other stuff on the discs, I had lost track of what year some of the funny moments happened.

The next scene appeared showing the slate from Season Eight, Episode Five on the Goodwin's living room set. Behind the slate, I recognized the attractive young woman around eighteen or twenty years of age who starred a couple of times that year as an older friend from Robin's scout troop. She was wearing jeans, with a typical 1990s shirt. When the slate clapped and was removed from the frame, the actress walked in front of the couch where I was sitting. As the young woman approached the couch, Kyle started a countdown:

"Wait for it," said Kyle, "Four, three, two, one."

The young woman was nearly upon me when she tripped on something that couldn't be seen in the frame. Where the countdown would've reached "zero," the young woman stumbled down on me and elbowed me in a not-so-comfortable place. You can guess why this was an outtake. The audience roared with laughter. While yelping in pain, I was motioning franticly for the young lady to get up. The frame switched to the other camera that was focused on the front door stage right as it opened. Mom, Robin, and Debbie entered to see the crazy display on the couch. Robin became wide-eyed. Debbie's reaction was more of giggles than anything. Marian's expression was like any concerned mother finding her teenage son doing something that looked very inappropriate with a young woman on the living room couch.

Marian as Mom exclaimed, "David Goodwin! What do you think you're doing?"

"It's not what it looks like! Ooooooowww!"

The audience continued to roar with laughter as the dialogue continued. The young woman finally got up. Davey continued to show signs of pain and agony on the couch.

My son Joe and my nephew Alex decided to joke about the scene. Obviously, they understood more what was going on.

"Look at that!" laughed Joe. "Dad was after a girl!"

"Yeah, you really were after her!" laughed Alex.

"You silly boys!" I grumbled. "It was an accident…she tripped and fell…"

Joe interrupted, "What was she supposed to do since this was a mistake?"

"She was supposed to fall into Davey's lap on the couch much higher," I scoffed. "Instead, she accidentally tripped and elbowed me…"

Joe and Alex joked and laughed about the scene.

"Oooo…Daddy!" exclaimed my daughter Elizabeth. "That girl was going to take you away!" All five of the kids got into the laughter.

During this commotion, I caught a glimpse of Celeste and Staci looking oddly at each other. At the time, I didn't realize why. It was like both of them had experienced a trigger moment. Kyle had to pause the video. He and I had to step in and get the kids to quiet down so we could continue to watch more clips. When I glanced back toward Celeste and Staci, they were busy helping Kyle and me.

Before we knew it, the Christmas and New Year's holidays would pass. As the new debut date approached, my work schedule became very busy. I was flying in and out of Dallas to do motivation talks and some voice work in a few different places. It would be a month after the debut before I could have time to watch it. Mom had previewed the first couple of shows. Dad said that he couldn't watch them. He said that he would explain later, after I had a chance to watch them. They said they were waiting until I could be at home to let the kids watch the show. At the time, I didn't quite understand what they meant by that. My parents made decisions what we could or couldn't watch back in the day. I thought they were saying that they wanted me to do the honors to supervise my own kids and have that experience as a parent. Celeste made it home in February after spending several weeks in LA, taping the last part of the show's second season. She didn't let on about the storylines or the plots. She was honoring my request to be surprised.

Finally, my work schedule let up. I was planning to go home and watch the show with my family—until Jamie Cabarello requested to meet with me for lunch in Grapevine, Texas (just miles from the DFW Airport). This was the same Jamie Cabarello whom Staci and I befriended years ago in the special Alcohol Awareness Week episode of *"Goodwin Circle."* I didn't know FibreTainment's leadership or their moral beliefs. Celeste had obtained a special VIP access to the FibreTainment Web site as an employment benefit during the run of the show. It was unfortunate that I didn't have time at work or home during that first month of the first season's availability to watch any episode or get a synopsis. From what I could tell from FibreTainment's selection of shows, there were some titles that Jerry Knobele would've objected to airing on our old network. Again, this was a streaming service—not over-the-air broadcast TV and not cable TV.

Jamie Cabarello had been in New York the last few days visiting some of his East Coast clients who made regular trips to the West Coast. He had entered the agent business, however, he occasionally starred in a few TV movies. He would only star in the family-friendly variety, like Staci did and eventually Celeste would. He even starred in one of Staci's movies. He was stopping over in Grapevine to visit with one of his clients who chose to live in Texas rather than LA or New York. He said that he had some information that we needed to discuss. He didn't want to surprise me over the phone.

Being a native Texan, I suggested that he and I visit a local Whataburger in Grapevine. He had thought I would like to do something more formal and less public. I told him that it was very unlikely we would be recognized. My appearance had changed a lot over the last thirty years. Some people often didn't recognize me unless I told them my name. However, most locals were respectful when I would visit Texas during my *"Goodwin Circle"* days. Despite that, I was always on my guard.

To save Jamie the time attempting to find the restaurant, I drove to Grapevine and picked him up from his hotel. We drove to the nearest Whataburger. We dined in and chose a corner table.

"Jamie, if I ever get a chance to visit your home state of Indiana again," I said, "I'll make sure to ask you what you like at White Castle. I enjoyed my previous visits."

"That's a deal!" commended Jamie.

After receiving our food, we got into eating and to the discussion.

"What's this all about?" I asked. "What could you not tell me over the phone?"

Jamie answered, "Now that I've thought about it. I'm not sure if it was best having this discussion over lunch."

"We have already ordered. I'm not going to throw away a good lunch just for you to tell me something. I'm starving."

"I hope that you still have an appetite when I tell you," warned Jamie.

Puzzled, I said, "I'm so hungry right now. Very little is going to stop me. I've only had a cracker sandwich pack and a Coke at the voice-over studio this morning."

"It concerns the TV show *'Goodwin Circles Around Again.'*"

I listened as I enjoyed a big bite from my burger.

"Celeste and Staci reprised their roles? Right?" asked Jamie.

"Yes, everyone knows that. It's been in the news."

"Have you seen any of the shows or read about the plotlines?"

"I didn't want to know plotlines," I answered. "I told Celeste to not tell me anything. Then, my schedule got busy. I haven't had time to watch any of it. Mom and Dad suggested to not let the kids watch it."

"I'm not revealing any particular plotlines. The buzz in Tinseltown is that there's been some trouble."

"Jamie, I heard about the audience fight. Celeste told me there were some tensions on set."

"The show's in trouble. It's more than just the audience brawl that you were told."

I looked at Jamie bewildered. *The new show is in trouble?*

He continued, "The show…this show… *'Goodwin Circles Around Again'*…is in trouble."

"That isn't what I have seen in some of the blurbs on the Web. There's talk of renewing for another season."

"Terrence Forrester quit the show before the second pilot," said Jamie.

"Second pilot? Terrence quit? How'd I miss that? Celeste didn't tell me."

"They did a rush job to get a second pilot done."

"What happened?" I asked.

Jamie leaned forward. "Word has it, the studio audience hated the first pilot's storyline, it didn't work, according to Albert Jacobs."

I kept eating my food while Jamie continued. "Jacobs got involved in some of the rewrites. They made a bunch of last-minute changes. Terrence said 'no.' He wasn't going to stay if they were going to expect him to do and say some of the things his character would've had to say in the rewrites."

"What did they do?" I asked.

"They got one of the extras to stand in for his character, Robert, on the pilot. They were able to get a recast done before the actual first season episode. They turned the whole process around very quickly."

"Who'd they recast the role with?"

"A veteran comedian named Harry Pynchon," answered Jamie.

I had to think a minute who Harry Pynchon was. His name seemed familiar. Jamie explained, "He had a special last month on the Comedy Tonight cable channel."

"I think I know who he is. I'm having trouble remembering his face and what his comedy is like. I usually don't watch that channel."

"If you heard his routines, he would make some sailors look like saints."

I was stunned as Jamie continued. "Yeah, this guy will say anything and everything to get a laugh. He doesn't know any limits or boundaries—from tasteful to tasteless. He loves to get people riled up with his profanity. Crude and rude is his forte."

"Oh, Precious Lord!" Who made *that* casting call?"

"Albert Jacobs, himself," answered Jamie.

"Albert Jacobs?"

"It's not the first time something like this has happened."

"Not the first time?" I asked.

"Not on our show," assured Jamie, "but, on some of Jacobs's other shows, there've been some less-than-subtle jokes and stuff."

"I can't remember a show offhand. Then again, I haven't watched all of Albert's work."

"Remember a show in the 1990s called '*It's Our Time*' that aired on Wednesday nights on our network at 10:00 p.m. back in 1993?"

"No, I don't," I answered.

"Jerry absolutely hated that show. Albert tried to pepper that show with innuendo and other envelope-pushing jokes."

"Back then, I was going to my church's youth group. It met on Wednesday nights. Then, I was doing homework and going to bed."

"Albert went over Jerry's head to get that show on. Several of the network affiliates complained about the story content, character behavior, and other stuff. Many church groups protested about it. It made a lot of news. Some affiliates refused to air the show, especially in the rural Deep South."

"I can understand why some of the affiliates refused the show."

Jamie continued, "There's a story that on the fourth episode, the jokes and action were too adult even for that late time period. Our network and the stations that showed it were fined millions of dollars. The FCC wasn't pleased. Jerry was able to dump '*It's Our Time*' after that debacle. The studio nearly fired Albert Jacobs from '*Goodwin Circle*,' but some of the upper network brass felt enough damage had been done. Albert faced the situation and kept '*Goodwin Circle*' clean."

"We were only kids then." That's probably why I don't remember the *'It's Our Time'* scandal."

"That's likely it. We were kids then."

"Of course, 1993 was around the time that Staci, Mom, Dad, and I became Christians," I said, "They wouldn't have encouraged anyone to watch *'It's Our Time.'*"

"Now, a dirty-mouth unbeliever is recast in the grandfather character of Bobby Goodwin," griped Jamie. "It's just horrible."

"Anything else changed?" I asked.

"Marian Deavers only lasted to the fourth episode as Caroline. They wrote her out of the series. Marian couldn't stand Harry Pynchon's mouth and insults. Caroline's departure was briefly mentioned in the next episode. Caroline committed an off-screen suicide..."

I was in the middle of sucking soft drink through the straw and almost had a full mouth of drink. I spat into the aisle floor and coughed.

"Are you okay?"

"No..." I responded, "this is insane!"

"It gets worse..."

I listened in horror. Jamie continued, "Your character, Davey..."

"Yeah?"

"He divorced Debbie prior to the first episode. She caught him in their bed with another woman and kicked them out."

"Darn!" I pounded my fist on the table. "They didn't ever give me the decency to let me know the writers were planning to do this!"

"And the woman was Debbie's former scout troop den mother from the old show."

My mouth dropped open in disgust. "Eeww! The actress who played that scout den mother was at least twenty-five years older!"

"I'm just saying what I know."

"What is this? 'Circus of the Rejects'?"

"Apparently," said Jamie, "Albert Jacobs got some extra writers to add a bunch of gritty and edgy stuff."

"What about the kids?"

"Robin had to move back home. Debbie moved in as well because their respective marriages are in a mess. Robin and Debbie are out of control. They are drinking, cussing, lying, having on-again, off-again relationships. I don't even want to describe their kids' lives. I feel sorry for the child stars playing them."

"Staci and Celeste?" I asked. "How are they handling this?"

"That's why Staci has had her family move back to California. Celeste was a little worried that without Kyle and the kids, Staci might get in trouble..."

"The moral support. Poor Staci. Poor Celeste. What are we going to do?"

"There's talk that a third season might be in the works, but FibreTainment hasn't confirmed yet."

"Have Staci or Celeste been asked to do anything else compromising?"

"No nudity or sex stuff. There've been plenty of sex jokes, innuendo, implied off-screen fornication, drug use, lots of alcohol. There's not an episode that goes by without alcohol present."

"Oh no!"

"The first season, fourth episode involves them attending a frat party."

"A frat party?" I asked shocked, "I'd hate to ask why."

"They get this crazy idea to meet younger men. They participate in a drinking contest that gets really bizarre. Staci and Celeste run around really silly like they are drunk. The frat guys encourage it. The scene eventually fades to black. In the next scene, we return to the old family home place. There are a few other implied references to—"

I interrupted, "I get the idea."

"I snuck onto into a taping. Debbie took the Lord's name in vain at least three times in I think was a first season episode. Robin slipped in a few profane words. I don't know if that was planned, or if it was bleeped. Robin also took the Lord's name in vain in that same episode. I couldn't stand watching much more of it. It was very strange to hear Celeste and Staci using that language."

"Did Staci or Celeste see you?"

"I don't think so," Jamie said, "but, I witnessed an audience brawl."

"Anyone hurt?"

"Just some rowdy folks in the audience. The off-color humor set off the crowd."

"Wow, that's a first for our show," I said.

"I've heard some reports that Staci and Celeste aren't happy."

"I can imagine."

"Kyle left the set after the first episode taping. When the set was closed after the audience brawl, he wouldn't go back, even if they allowed him."

"Uh-oh, that sounds like Kyle. For him to walk out on the production like that, that's trouble."

"He doesn't like to see her around other men—kissing and such."

"Is Celeste kissing other guys?"

"No, she's said to have put her foot down that she wouldn't give any to the guys…or the gals."

I responded with wide eyes. "There's been… Okay. I'm glad that Celeste said no to that."

"Staci is kissing only guys. Unfortunately, some of the guest stars and minor characters…"

"I get the idea."

"Unfortunately, they're locked in a contract. If FibreTainment renews for a third season, I don't know if they'll be able to change the show."

"And their contract requires them to promote the show," I said. "They can't say anything negative. Any hint of negative comments…"

Jamie answered, "Like asking fans to forgive them or saying they are sorry might be enough to cause legal ramifications."

"We may need to get some lawyers to look at those contracts."

"There've been some reports that Staci has been heard crying in her dressing room on some days during lunch breaks. Staci and Celeste have been seen crying in Staci's car after a taping day."

"They really put up a good front the last time I was out there during the holidays. Although, I could tell Celeste wanted to tell me something, but she looked like she couldn't."

"Remember, that's good acting."

"Me and my big mouth to tell her that I didn't want to know the plotlines before seeing the finished product. I'm a terrible husband."

"You didn't know this was going to happen," reassured Jamie.

"Two well-known artists who are Christians—"

Jamie corrected, "You mean two well-known Christians who are actresses."

"I never imagined seeing this."

"We don't have a Jerry Knobele to stop this or a Standards and Practices department to review the content."

"Wow, I haven't heard anything in the news about the show."

"You have to search for it. Mainstream critics have panned the show. The Christian Websites and blogs have been raising questions about what's going on. Staci and Celeste are getting a bunch of complaints."

"I'm surprised no one at church has said anything about it. I've had no calls."

"I'm sure word has gotten around. With the show on FibreTainment, it's taking a while for some folks to find time for it."

"No one would tell me?" I asked.

"You haven't starred on a TV series in the last ten years. You told Celeste not to tell you any plotlines. If any of her close church friends asked about it, she probably told them what you told her. If any of them had found the show and told you, would you've believed it?"

"I can't understand why our pastors or elders didn't call," I said.

Jamie said, "Maybe they know. Think about it."

"Why not tell me?"

"They know you've been busy. They know you've been in and out of town over the last several months. They know Celeste is California."

"I've spent several Sundays in California with Celeste. The kids have gone with me a few times."

"Your closer friends at church may know what's going on. Celeste may have called your church for counseling or guidance."

"Not to tell me?"

"She may have said you would be upset if this was revealed. She had promised not to reveal storylines to you. If anyone had questions, the church would take care of it."

"We've tried to be private at church."

"Staci posted a promotional photo of them a few days before the debut on her social media account. Some of the fans questioned what was going on. Some fans hinted that something was amiss. Comments went from critical of the skimpiness of the clothing, to she and Celeste were going to Hell, claiming their salvation was false—calling them false converts."

I shook my head as Jamie continued, "Staci got mad. She posted telling both sides to stop. They wouldn't until she removed the picture."

"Staci has been very committed to family-oriented, family-values entertainment. From what you are describing, it appears she may have been forced into compromising."

"I've had some friends on the inside tell me that she has tried to kindly request removing various jokes and other content. If she hadn't, it would've been much worse."

"Much worse?"

Jamie answered, "The writers, various directors, Albert Jacobs, and some of the FibreTainment suits aren't allowing Staci or Celeste to get rid of all of it. The suits think the trashy stuff sells. There are other shows out there doing a bunch of stuff like this."

I shook my head again. "This is awful."

"Another source is claiming that the writers are pulling from 'real life' and 'the culture.'"

"Where did they get these writers? A bunch of juvenile delinquents?"

"If they can write, they hire. Albert Jacobs has been the kingpin on this one. He isn't quite the same man he was thirty years ago."

"I think he may be the same man but only thirty years more of filth and baggage," I grumbled, "that has encouraged him to pull my wife and my sister into this 'sleaze-fest show' and tarnish their reputations. We're going to have to get some lawyers involved."

"Another issue is many fan blogs have raised questions about the show's content. The show is rated TV-G!"

I asked puzzled, "TV-G?!"

"Yep."

"With all of that junk?"

"Yep."

"This isn't a sequel to *'Goodwin Circle'*," I moaned. "This is 'Sodom and Gomorrah Live' taped before a studio audience!"

"Was taped before a studio audience until the audience brawl. Reports are circulating that kids are really having a field day with the show."

"A TV-G show shouldn't have sex jokes, anything sexual, profanity, and such content. TV-PG or a TV-14 rated show is most likely to have it, but not TV-G."

"People are going back to see what Staci said in 2014. This show would be a 'family-friendly' show."

"Something changed," I said.

"Celeste claimed in a recent interview that *'Goodwin Circles Around Again'* would be appropriate for the whole family to watch."

"Not *our* family!" I protested. "Not with the content you describe. She must've been fed a set of lines to say. This is just wrong."

"Some of my friends out in Hollywood think this is acceptable for a streaming TV show."

"The suits at FibreTainment should be ashamed of themselves."

"Unfortunately, no one's organizing anything to deal with it," said Jamie.

"We may have to do something."

"I'll get some lawyers involved," Jamie said. "They might be able to find a way to stop this."

"There's one thing for sure, we're going to have to be much more careful next time to prevent something like this from happening again."

"I'm also afraid what influence all of this junk could have on a believer. You know 1 Corinthians 15:31-34 says." Jamie pulled out his phone and turned to an online Bible and read, "*I affirm, brethren, by the boasting in you which I have in Christ Jesus our Lord, I die daily. If from human motives I fought with wild beasts at Ephesus, what does it profit me? If the dead are not raised, let us eat and drink, for tomorrow we die.* **Do not be deceived: 'Bad company corrupts good morals.'** *Become sober-minded as* *you ought, and stop sinning; for some have no knowledge of God. I speak this to your shame."* [NASB]

"Staci and Celeste know better," I said. "Even for strong believers, they're right in the Lion's Den. They're being used as pawns in someone's devilish game."

"Devilish is the right word for this," agreed Jamie.

"Not to mention what havoc this is causing for families around the country...or around the world."

"FibreTainment is planning to distribute this show and other shows on a worldwide basis."

"Poor Staci and Celeste," I muttered. "That means that just leaving the country wouldn't help..."

"Unless it's in a remote part of the world with no Internet."

"All those families—many of them trusted Staci and Celeste before they made any promotions. They have been the most family-caring people I know. I married Celeste. I know Staci and Celeste's Christian walk. Celeste became a Christian not long after I did. I helped her."

"Celeste and Staci are trying to stop the enemy's work," reassured Jamie, "but they're outnumbered."

"They don't have the power to remove all of it, unfortunately."

"Don't be completely dismayed. God knows Staci's and Celeste's hearts. They're His. They've been His children for many years."

"I hope that neither of them crack under the strain," I said. "Obviously, this is going to require some careful and caring prayers."

"God is using them behind the scenes to show that His Will won't allow this show to succeed. With all of this simulated debauchery, He won't."

"For the young believers, I hope and pray that no one stumbles as a result of this. Matthew 18:6 comes to mind."

Jamie searched for other Bible verses on his phone. "I agree. As you know, Mark and Luke have a similar verse." *Mark 9:42* and *Luke 17:2*.

I looked at my watch. "My food's getting cold. We need to get done. When is your flight to LA?"

"I'm staying tonight here in Grapevine at that hotel where you picked me up. I have one client I'm visiting later today. Then, I'll get some sleep tonight and fly out tomorrow morning."

We finished our food. While finishing our conversation, I helped a server clean up the mess I had made. After lunch, I drove Jamie back to the hotel. After that, I called the studio to say I wouldn't be coming back that afternoon because something had come up. I started driving around Frisco and Plano for the next few hours.

How was I going to tell Celeste that I knew what had been going on? At least I knew before being completely surprised by all of the terrible stuff. Celeste really kept a good poker face during our Christmas visit and some of the other visits I made to LA while Staci and Celeste were acting in this show. I also found it too hard to believe how little press this show was getting, other than a few talk shows. No one was really trying to address the content issues. Whenever questions were raised about bad critical reviews and upset fans, Staci and her other co-stars would discount the naysayers.

Then, again, this isn't the same as it was thirty years ago when we had only a few broadcast channels, no Internet, no streaming services, and limited access to trade publications. Now, the Internet has made this information available to the masses. Anyone could become a critic with a blog site and a TubeVideo channel. I mulled in my mind what I was going to say to Celeste, who had returned home a few days ago. I was very uncertain what was going to happen next. I knew my faith was being tested more than ever. I knew very well that Staci and Celeste were in grave danger. I was scared. I knew that God was trying to keep my heart still and tell me not to worry. I wasn't sure what would happen next.

5

THE CONFESSION AND THE
AFTERMATH HITS AT HOME

◆———————◆———————◆

During my afternoon drive, my thoughts swirled about the public perception of Celeste's and Staci's Christian walks with the new revelation of the show's controversies. I also thought about our loyal fans that were deceived by the new show's mislabeled television rating. Staci's name had become synonymous with "high-quality family entertainment." My wife, whom I'd loved for over twenty years and whom I had never known to intentionally hurt anyone in all that time, weighed very heavily on my mind. Did any of our Christian fans become disillusioned in the faith because of this show? Did Staci or Celeste—or both—cause unintentional stumbling blocks by their participation and behavior both on and off the set? I knew that I was going to have to figure out a way to break the news to Celeste what I knew. As I entered my office, Celeste called me.

"Hey, sweetie!"

"Mike, where are you?" asked Celeste. "The family tracking app shows you were all over Frisco and Plano the last couple of hours."

"I'm home now. I had to drive out to Grapevine."

"Grapevine? Why?"

"Jamie Caballero is in the area. He flew in today from New York. He had some business with a client today after we had lunch. Darn! I forgot to ask him who."

"So you drove to meet with him?" asked Celeste.

"Yep. We got a Whataburger and talked about old times and current business trends."

"Elizabeth, Joe, and Carmen want to give us a date night since you and I haven't had much time alone together. Elizabeth agreed to watch those two. They're going over to a neighbor's house to watch a movie."

Celeste said, "I'm at least forty minutes away. Traffic is heavy out here. Your dad met us in Dallas late this afternoon. Your mom is riding with him."

"I see you on the GPS. I could order some dinner, and we can spend some time together."

"If it's the usual place."

"I'll pick it up," I said, "so y'all can come home."

"I feel like you've done plenty of driving this afternoon."

I ordered dinner for two from our favorite restaurant in Plano. I got through the Friday afternoon rush hour traffic, picked up the food, and arrived back home. Celeste had just arrived. The kids had left for the neighbor's. After fixing our plates, we enjoyed our meal together.

After eating, we made our way to our living room sofa. I suggested to Celeste that we watch something on TV. She wasn't sure what to choose. It suddenly hit me. *Is this really the way I want to treat her after a wonderful dinner-for-two? Make her watch "Goodwin Circles Around Again" with me? It might seem like a dirty trick. This might be the best way to confront her without getting into accusations. Is she truly proud of the show, or is she ashamed? Making her watch it with me will put her on the spot to see her true motives. Can she really handle all the "trash" she and Staci helped create for the viewing masses?*

I said to Celeste, "You know what? I haven't had a chance to see your new show."

"You haven't?"

"I've been so busy, I haven't had a chance for the kids and me to watch it."

"Why now?" asked Celeste.

"I got some encouragement to view it. We have that FibreTainment subscription you received."

"Are you sure you want to watch that show?"

"Yesss."

"I need to explain some things before we watch..."

"What's there to explain? Remember, you promised to let me watch it without giving me any of the plot."

"You read the first pilot script."

"That's months ago," I said. "What...first pilot?"

"The show had some changes since the first pilot," admitted Celeste. "Did anyone tell you?"

"They might've."

"Did you read about it in the news, or did someone tell you?" inquired Celeste.

"I might've heard about a second pilot being shot, but you're right. That can happen. I've seen shows change for various reasons. Even *'Goodwin Circle'* had some changes from its pilot. I'm determined to use the time right now to watch a couple of episodes. I had someone tell me to watch at least four particular episodes."

"Someone you know has seen it?"

"Yeees, the show's been out for a month."

"I'm not sure that this is the best time to watch this," cautioned Celeste. "I've developed this urge to not watch myself."

"What?" I egged, "That's not like you." *I knew it!* Her expression told me she didn't want me to watch or be in the same room while I watched it.

"I'm a little concerned that you're not going to like some of the changes that were made."

"Now, Celeste, I'm a grown adult. I've watched movies and TV in the past. Some of it wasn't good. When it got bad, I turned it off or walked out."

"Could I ask that we pray and have us put on the Full Armor of God?" begged Celeste.

I looked at her, surprised. I knew deep down she was feeling guilty; it was written across her face. Her poker face was slipping. I played along.

"This is your show. An updated version of our old show *'Goodwin Circle'* now called *'Goodwin Circles Around Again.'* What could possibly be wrong with a clean, wholesome show?"

"I really insist we pray before watching it," Celeste pleaded.

"Ok, if it'll help ease your mind. You're my wife. I'll honor your wishes."

We bowed our heads, and Celeste began, "Dear Lord. As we prepare to watch this TV show that Staci and I participated in, I humbly ask that we prepare our hearts and minds what Michael is about to see. I need to get my Bible to read this, pardon me, Lord."

Celeste reached for our Bible on the coffee table and thumbed through the pages to Ephesians 6:10-18. The Armor of God.

Celeste continued, "Lord, please guard us with your Armor. Written in Ephesians 6:10-18: *'Finally, be strong in the Lord and in the strength of His might. Put on the full armor of God, so that you will be able to stand firm against the schemes of the devil. For our struggle is not against flesh and blood, but against the rulers, against the powers, against the world forces of this darkness, against the spiritual forces of wickedness in the heavenly places. Therefore, take up the full armor of God, so that you will be able to resist in the evil day, and having done everything, to stand firm. Stand firm therefore, having girded your loins with truth, and having put on the breastplate of righteousness, and having shod your feet with the preparation of the gospel of peace; in addition to all, taking up the shield of faith with which you will be able to extinguish all the flaming arrows of the evil one. And take the helmet of salvation, and the sword of the Spirit, which is the word of God. With all prayer and petition pray at all times in the Spirit, and with this in view, be on the alert with all perseverance and petition for all the saints, and pray on my behalf, that utterance may be given to me in the opening of my mouth, to make known with boldness the mystery of the gospel, for which I am an ambassador in chains; that in proclaiming it I may speak boldly, as I ought to speak.'* [NASB]"

"Michael, do you agree to have the Armor on?" asked Celeste.

"Of course," I answered. "For you, sweetie, yes."

"Please protect my husband and me what we'll see and hear. As we watch Staci and I give life to these…classic…characters as adults…please forgive me for what I have done, for what many fans have had to endure, and for when this whole situation is over, I pray that I'll be able to reconcile with fans and family. In Jesus's Holy Name we pray. Amen."

When I opened my eyes, I looked at Celeste with puzzlement. She could tell that I was very surprised by her prayer.

"Wasn't that a bit strong for a family-friendly sitcom?" I asked.

"I wanted to make sure that you and I were protected from what we're about to see," quivered Celeste.

"You're making it sound like y'all did a dirty movie."

"Let's get this over with."

I turned on the TV and navigated to the FibreTainment app. We finally found the *"Goodwin Circles Around Again"* choice. While searching, I noticed that *"Goodwin*

Circle" was also available. As I looked at the screen, I noticed the TV-G rating on the new show.

As I navigated the Family TV Show Section, I heard a familiar voice guide us through the menus. I suddenly remembered that FibreTainment had contracted with my voice-over company to record these sound clips for their software menus and a few promotions. I exclaimed with false joy to Celeste that it was my voice on those sound clips. Later, I told her I hoped no one would recognize my voice.

When selecting the first episode, I heard my recorded voice announce, "You have chosen *'Goodwin Circles Around Again*: Season One, Episode One.'" After activating the episode, the FiberTainment logo displayed on the screen. Then, my recorded recitation included the following words as they flew onto the screen, "FiberTainment. We put the *Family* in *Family Entertainment!*" Finally, this screen faded and eventually onto the show. During all of this, I pondered legal remedies I could pursue to make FibreTainment stop using my voice after this situation. At this point, I thought to myself a new slogan, "FibreTainment. We *take* the *Family out* of *Family Entertainment!*"

I recognized the familiar theme song from *"Goodwin Circle"* but updated. Each of the stars appeared at the beginning with their own title cards. I didn't let on to Celeste that I had been forewarned what I was about to see. I wouldn't get into reciting all of the storyline. The episode started rather innocently. As it progressed, it wouldn't take very long for the disturbing elements to enter.

Harry Pynchon walked into the living room set of Robert and Caroline Goodwin's old TV home. He looked too young for the part. Marian Deavers walked in. I could tell that something looked off in her acting. Harry's lack of chemistry with Marian showed in the episode. She looked more frightened than affectionate. Suddenly, Harry began spouting a line with his first of several expletives. He showed a lot of pride in how many such words he could say. Marian was very nervous with the dialogue. Staci and Celeste eventually walked in and gave their lines explaining the troubles that their characters were in. When Celeste—as Debbie—revealed that my character Davey had been caught in an inappropriate relationship and chased from the house, the audience roared with laughter.

Celeste as Debbie threw a disparaging line about Davey that included cussing. Debbie said, "The divorce papers are on their way."

The audience members continued whooping, clapping, and laughing with catcalls with every expletive, dirty joke, and sexual innuendo that happened in the first few minutes of the show. I couldn't believe what I was seeing and hearing. Was this really a "family-friendly show" for the 2010s? Sitting in the same room with my lovely Christian wife and having her there to relive the episode on this side of the screen made the situation seem awkward. I could tell that she wasn't happy.

I kept turning to her when more filthy language uttered from her lips as Debbie. Every time it happened, the audience seemed to catcall as if they were getting more fuel to drive their thrill fire. It seemed the audience knew this Christian actress was giving her first worldly performance by trashing the Ten Commandments left and right. Celeste shook her head and tears began to fall. She acted like—and I felt like—spiritually she was dying inside. I finally had to stop the show.

Finally, Celeste started crying which progressed to sobbing. I quickly reached over to her and hugged her. I was also tearing up from all that I had seen. I couldn't believe it. I witnessed her—in character—use language I rarely heard from her in real life. She took the Lord's name in vain three different ways in the first fifteen minutes of the half-hour show.

"I tried," sobbed Celeste, "I really tried to stop it. They wouldn't let me."

"Who wouldn't let you?" I asked.

"The writers. They played all sorts of games with us. Staci tried to negotiate. She tried to keep calm." She sniffed. "I tried to follow her example. I finally had to complain. The writers...Albert Jacobs. They created all sorts of so-called compromises to reduce the content. They had no intent on cleaning it up." I cradled her head next to my shoulder.

Celeste had been pulled into a really difficult situation. I hugged her for several minutes while we let the tears flow. One thing that was very certain to me: Celeste finally felt relieved of all this held-back stress. Having to relive the scenes was too much to bear. For the first time, I had witnessed my beautiful bride encourage Psalms 51 and have her within my arms.

"Celeste, you don't have to say anything. You've said plenty in your prayer. Your reaction tells me that you didn't want this to happen. You've been forgiven. I also forgive you. Jamie Caballero told me about the show. He warned me. I'm so sorry that I had to put you through this. I won't make you watch this again. I know you tried. I now know that you wanted to tell me so badly in December. No more waiting to see the show later. Why did they do this?"

"They saw an opportunity to use us; I can only guess," said Celeste, as I wiped my tears.

"Forcing a Christian into a compromising situation and holding money and a contract like that isn't fair," I said. "At some point, we need to talk to Staci. I understand that she was also emotionally stressed through this experience. There's word circulating that Staci locked herself in during one lunch break and cried her eyes out."

"We had more than one occasion where we left the studio and cried our eyes out in the car."

"I heard that too. I'm also concerned how long Staci can handle this. Is she being the same way as you? Your heart cracked having to relive it. You so desperately wanted to tell; I wouldn't let you."

"I know she isn't too thrilled. She was so glad when the last day of taping happened on the second season. Now, the editors are working on the second season episodes for distribution in the fall."

For the rest of the evening, we spent time together. I suggested maybe *"Goodwin Circle"* for old time's sake. Celeste didn't feel like it. She admitted that it was very difficult now to watch the original show, knowing the new show's ugliness. Instead, I found our DVD copy of *"Goodwin Circle"* and decided to replay some of the blooper clips. Celeste felt the blooper clips would be better with the breaking-the-fourth-wall moments. I played again that crazy blooper with her playing Debbie for the first time in the scouting outfit and my front doorknob debacle.

The kids came home later. Elizabeth, Joe, and Carmen were in a festive mood. They had enjoyed their time at the neighbor's. Joe and Carmen were discussing bedtime. As they walked to their bedrooms, the kids danced and sang. As they started, Celeste suddenly looked worried.

"What is it?" I asked.

"They've seen the show. That song and dance is from an episode when Robin and Debbie attended a wild frat party."

"Uh-oh!"

"Kids, stop that!" scolded Celeste. "Stop that song and dance!"

"Why?" said Elizabeth.

"It's just wrong!" clamored Celeste.

"Mom, everyone is talking about it at school," said Elizabeth.

"The three of you don't need to be singing or imitating it!" exclaimed Celeste.

"I find that strange, Mom," said Joe. "You and Aunt Staci were on there doing it. A lot of the kids said that it was cool when Aunt Staci cussed."

"I'm surprised, too, Mom," admitted Elizabeth. "You had the guts to yell a lot of bad words."

"Mom?" innocently asked Carmen. "What's cussing and what's a bad word."

"Stop it! That's enough!" scolded Celeste. "You can't say those words in this house!"

I shook my head. "Three strikes in a row!"

I motioned the kids to the living room sofa. "Alright, that's enough! All three of you, quiet!" I exclaimed, "I'll ask the questions, and I want some answers!"

I explained to the kids, using abbreviations for the unacceptable words they had said. "You'll not use God's name as a curse word or with any of those dirty words in this house again. You'll not dishonor Him, Jesus, the Holy Spirit—The Trinity—or any of Their names! Dishonoring them is against the Ten Commandments—the Third Commandment to be exact. *[Exodus 20:7]*. Where did you get those words?"

"Mom and Aunt Staci are all the rage at school," quipped Elizabeth.

"The guys are all laughing at the words," piped Joe. "Some of the kids already know them."

"Elizabeth, what do you mean by 'Mom and Aunt Staci are all the rage at school?'" I asked.

"Some of the other kids are wowed that Mom and Aunt Staci would say those things," Elizabeth admitted. "Those words. Some of the kids are using them when talking with each other."

"Look! Where did you see Mom and Aunt Staci doing this?" I asked.

"On TV," answered Carmen.

"Where did you see this?" I pried.

"Tonight at the neighbor's while we let you have your date night," answered Elizabeth.

"You watched this on FibreTainment?" I asked. "At the neighbor's tonight?"

"Yep. The guys think Mom and Aunt Staci are hot!" joked Joe. "Some of the guys wondered if Aunt Staci was really drunk during those binge-drinking scenes. Those frat party guys had fun! If that is what college is like, I may want to see what a frat is all about."

"What's a frat?" asked Carmen.

I looked at Celeste as I paced in front of the kids on what to do.

"Alright. FibreTainment is off-limits to you from this point forward," I said. "You don't watch anything on that service without my permission. No Internet access for a week. If you need it for school, Mom or I must supervise. That is for all of you—including you, Elizabeth! Internet access is restricted in the first place, but this situation involving this TV show is unacceptable. All three of you will ask God to forgive you of the behavior you presented. You're not to use those profane words at school, at home, or around anyone. I don't care what the other kids think. It's disrespectful. Also, no movies at the neighbor's for a month."

"You must understand. That TV show isn't real," said Celeste to the kids. "I was in an acting role. It wasn't supposed to be me."

"It looked like you and Aunt Staci were having fun doing it," quipped Joe.

"Enough," I exclaimed, "Aunt Staci and Mom made a big mistake. They regret saying those things. They weren't in their right mind when those statements and words were said. You'll not repeat or sing those bad words, again."

"That's no fun. Aunt Staci says stuff like that to 'her kids' on the show," Joe said, "but she does the same thing behind their backs."

"Don't talk back to me," I answered. "The show isn't real. Mom and Aunt Staci did wrong. Celeste, I'll have to make an example of you to the kids."

"An example?" asked Celeste.

"Celeste, you don't get to use Internet for a week unless I supervise it. You need to ask for forgiveness to the kids for your inappropriate behavior on that program. All three of you aren't allowed to watch it even if Mom and Aunt Staci are all the rage. They made a mistake...a BIG mistake! If you talk like that again, you're getting worse punishment!" I exclaimed.

The kids accepted their punishments. Celeste begged for forgiveness. The kids responded that they forgave their mom. They finally went off to bed. We heard them praying that night to God asking for forgiveness for their behavior. I felt sorry for the kids being deceived. If Staci and Celeste had not been the cause, each of them could've received worse.

"I can't imagine how the other parents are dealing with this," I said.

"The kids didn't even care if they were characters or us," said Celeste.

"You gave life to Debbie by putting on a 'costume.' You put on the Debbie 'costume' to become Debbie. You gave Debbie life. But Debbie isn't real. God actually gave life to you, Celeste Hernandez, my wife. You did all of those actions—not just the character!"

"That's a strange way of describing it."

"If this is getting around the school, you can imagine that it's going around town and elsewhere. I wonder why no one before now has said anything to me."

"Maybe some people aren't aware of it? Knowing you all these years, I doubt folks would want to muster up the courage to tell you."

"Actually, I've had a couple of folks want to talk about the show, but I told them I didn't want to talk about it. 'No spoilers, please.'"

"Word probably got around that you wanted to see it first to make your own decision."

"Some people know that I don't like to read any spoilers if they appear in the trades. Some folks may think I want to record and watch all of those interviews. Both of our schedules have been very busy. With all of the traveling and work, I haven't wanted to sit down and watch TV…or go back and watch stuff."

Celeste checked on the kids while I researched what the critics and fans were saying about the show. I poured through the search engine results. Some secular sites were praising the show a bit, while many more blasted it. Some Christian blogs and Web sites were questioning why Staci and Celeste were doing all of this debauchery, profanity, drunkenness, and crudeness on the show.

Staci's and Celeste's social media accounts were getting split commentary about the show's content and questioning their decisions to participate. Fans were arguing back and forth, taking sides either liking or hating the show. My social media account had fan posts asking why I would let Celeste do this show and if her Christian beliefs were a total fabrication. All three of us were seeing posts calling us "hypocrites," "false converts," and "double-minded." I even found reviews and comments as far as Australia. Pictures and show descriptions were spreading like wildfire across the Internet. This wasn't looking good at all. Celeste and I prayed to God that our families would weather this storm.

6

THE AFTERMATH HITS THE LOCAL CHURCH AND BEYOND

❖───────❖───────❖

After our experience on Friday night, Celeste and I had come to terms with the show. I had trouble shaking the disappointment that I felt. I had texted Staci that something had happened Friday night. I told her that things got very emotional concerning the show. Staci, on the other hand, was a little less expressive about it. I could only assume that she didn't have time to think about it. I noticed online that some of her fans had posted comments about her, but she wasn't responding very much. Of course, she had been very busy with different projects.

I realized some might ask. *Why didn't you call her immediately and condemn her actions?* While some might say that is what I should've done. I knew Staci better than most. When I was younger, I did that once. That was a big mistake. Staci and I had grown up since then. Calling her up to chew her out was not a solution. Staci was getting enough fan expression. I didn't want to add salt to an already festering wound.

I didn't have much time to text Staci the details. As the days progressed, more items presented themselves. By Monday, I happened to be home during the weekday. For some reason, I had the TV on InterCable News in my home office. I simply watched the different news stories fly by. Then, a breaking news alert appeared. What came next was a real shock.

The TV news anchor said, "A fraternity party in the west central Tennessee town of Valley Grove, turned tragic for one student. We have received this report."

The channel switched to video footage as a voice-over reporter said, "A fraternity party has resulted in at least one major injury and numerous arrests at the campus of Valley Grove College. Authorities are investigating the local Delta Alpha fraternity. Members had built a large wall of branches and shrub debris to obscure views around the perimeter of the party site.

Campus police report that over 200 people were in attendance at the event. The apparent centerpiece involved a drinking contest. At some point during the party, two female students began a drinking frenzy. Both students' names are currently being withheld until a full investigation can be completed.

According to preliminary reports, one of the female students—at approximately 10:25 p.m. Friday night—collapsed and became unresponsive. This resulted in paramedics and campus police being called to the scene. Campus police called for additional officers and crowd control when it became apparent that a potential riot situation could ensue. Several students and guests appeared to be in various states of intoxication. Police are attempting to determine who might be responsible for the alcohol. School regulations prohibit alcohol consumption on-campus, including Greek events.

The unidentified female student was immediately airlifted to an unidentified Memphis hospital. Officials reported on Monday, the student remained unresponsive at this time, on life support. As we learn more on this story, we will try to bring you updates as they become available."

The channel switched to a news anchor in Los Angeles. This news anchor read, "In a somewhat related story, some of the party's organizers claim that the drinking binge contest was inspired by a recent episode of the FibreTainment TV reboot series *'Goodwin Circles Around Again.'* Some viewers may recall that this series is an updated version of the 1980s sitcom *'Goodwin Circle,'* that starred sister-brother duo Staci and Mike Whitman. A recent episode storyline of the new series featured Staci Whitaker-Carella and Mike Whitman's wife, Celeste Hernandez, involved in a wild fraternity party stunt. The new series began its first season in February. The second season is expected to release later this year. InterCable News has attempted to receive comment from FibreTainment studio representatives, and the actors involved. No comments and responses have been received at this time."

I located the news story on the InterCable News site and shared it with our family members by text. Celeste responded with a crying face. Staci responded with prayer hands. As that day progressed, my thoughts were on the young female college student lying in that hospital bed barely clinging to life. While I read a few e-mails, I received a phone call from our church.

Justin Lockwood, one of our care pastors, called. He shared, "Mike, a couple of church discipline issues have come to our attention."

"Church discipline issues?" I asked surprised.

"Yes, will you and Celeste be available for me to visit you at home this evening?"

"Yes, but could we just discuss this over the phone?"

"I don't want to get into specifics," said Justin. "We're still getting some of the details. One involves an incident at our Main Campus. The other is out of state."

"Okay. Would 7:00 p.m. be good?"

"Yes."

"We'll see you this evening."

I had a hunch what was this was about. I told Celeste to be prepared. Around seven, Justin arrived and parked out front. As he approached the front door, I could tell that his expression was one of concern.

I greeted him at the door. We made our way to the living room. Celeste and I sat on the sofa, and Justin sat in the nearby lounge chair.

"What's happening?" I asked.

"We have a couple of issues," said Justin.

"I think I may know what this might involve," I said, "but, I'll let you tell us what you know."

Justin looked a little surprised, "You do? Let's see if this is what you think this is. The first one involves an incident that happened in our Children's Ministry last Sunday, in our 6th grade class."

"Okay," I said, "what's happened?"

"It hasn't been an isolated incident in that particular class," said Justin. "We've had several students singing songs and making references to various profane words, gestures, and mannerisms."

"That's strange. It's not any of our kids?" I said. "At least, I hope it's not."

"No," said Justin. "We've had some allegations that the sources of the songs and behavior are connected to family you have on a TV show."

"My family?" I asked.

"Yes," Justin answered.

"As I said, I suspect I know what this is about," I said. "I think I know which show this is and who in my family is on it. But, we have such a large congregation. How do they know Celeste and I are members here?"

"Easy," said Justin. "Celeste posted sometime back that she attended one of the church events on her social media. Someone recognized her. In turn, the pastoral staff and I checked the records. You and Celeste have been here for a while."

"Oops," said Celeste. "I just started back acting again."

Justin responded, "You need to be careful what you post."

"So what can we do about this situation?" I asked.

"You and Celeste have connections to this whole phenomenon, the *'Goodwin Circle'* TV show."

I clarified, "But this is about the new show that just released."

"Yes," said Justin. "It seems to be spreading like wildfire. A bunch of kids are running around mimicking the show. Some of the visuals and language are being recited by kids as young as *ten*...at our church."

"I'm not on the new show...yet," I said.

Justin answered, "You have two family members that are."

I said, "Staci lives in California."

"But, Celeste lives here," said Justin.

"What are you recommending?" I asked. "Attempting to discipline Celeste over this?"

"We're trying to find a way to stop it," said Justin. "I figured that you could shed some insight into what has caused this?"

"We're closer to the source, and you think that we can stop it?" asked Celeste.

"Or help us figure out why this is happening," said Justin.

"Have you watched the show?" I asked.

"No, we've had some parents who have," said Justin. "It's been a mixed reception. Some like it. There's a growing number that don't."

"I'm surprised that this one show is gaining this much traction," I said.

"Depends on the show, and what the general public is watching and viewing," said Justin. "With the general public aware that you are Christians adds another issue to the mix."

"We've encountered a problem at the studio, or Celeste and Staci have," I said. "They're being used. The show heads are peddling this stuff."

"That's what the ministry team and elders suspected," said Justin, "which is why we didn't rush to judgment."

"I'm concerned our reputations could be at stake," said Celeste. "Since we are believers, our participation could become a stumbling block for many, especially young Christians. I'm not sure if my sister-in-law is really aware of the ramifications."

"Justin, we learned that Staci posted a picture to her social media page a few weeks ago."

"It included a cast photo of our TV family," said Celeste.

"Fans were told that the show would be 'family-friendly' and an update of the older show," I said.

Justin said, "I remember watching *'Goodwin Circle'* back in the day."

"Staci and I promoted that prior to taping the first pilot episode," said Celeste. "After the first pilot was rejected, someone at FibreTainment decided to do a rushed revamped pilot with profanity, innuendo, and such. The second pilot sold."

"I see," said Justin. "The ministry team and elders suspected something had happened."

"Staci and I are locked into contracts to promote the show until FibreTainment decides to end it," said Celeste.

"Do you have a copy of the picture that was posted?" asked Justin.

Celeste looked on her smartphone and showed the picture to Justin.

"Okay. What was the problem?" asked Justin.

"Within minutes of its posting, fans of Staci's page began debating back and forth whether her attire was appropriate," said Celeste. "It went much further than that."

"Okay," said Justin. "After looking at that dress, it's somewhat short."

"Other fans started getting concerned over the dress being too showy," said Celeste, "then, people were calling her salvation into question."

"Celeste, please keep in mind that Staci may see nothing wrong with this dress," said Justin. "It's a little short and rather showy. Modesty can be a debatable issue in some situations."

"I'm sure," I said.

"There are some people that would say that this dress isn't terrible," commented Justin. "On the other hand, there are some Christians who hold much more conservative views. In their minds, this would be too short, in some circles."

"It might be okay in Los Angeles," I said.

"Yes, and even Dallas. In other parts of the state, you might get a very different reaction," said Justin. "How did she respond to the fans when they got mad?"

"She got angry at both sides," said Celeste. "She later went on and said that she didn't care what the masses thought."

Justin shook his head. "That's not good. That would be a typical human response, but that isn't a biblical response."

"What would be considered a biblical response?" I asked.

"For times when there is no clear biblical answer, Romans 14 and 15 would be the best way to handle it. Romans 14:1-12 means that we should not be condemning or judging fellow believers when their convictions—stricter convictions—differ from ours," said Justin. "Romans 14:13-23 means that we shouldn't be on the other side to use our freedom to encourage or pressure another believer to sin and violate one's own conscience."

"In other words, the first half of Romans 14 would apply to the fans in this case," I said. "They shouldn't have rushed to judgment by condemning Staci for the picture post and the shortness of the dress. Is that right?"

"Correct," said Justin.

"The other half of Romans 14 would've applied to Staci," said Celeste. "She should've apologized for the picture."

"She could've apologized," said Justin. "If she merely removed the post and said nothing, she shouldn't have become angry at both sides in the argument that ensued."

"Many fans have come to know the three of us for a certain public image," said Celeste. "To do something on the public stage that would appear to compromise our beliefs, it's caused some to react terribly. There are many out there who may be ready to assume that Staci and I are false converts or are simply compromising our faith."

"The public only knows the public persona that they've seen," I said, "There are too many for them to know us as the real us."

"Everybody wants to be your friend," said Justin. "You can't possibly do that. Most people have a few close friends. Some people who want to be your friend sometimes can have ulterior motives."

"Unfortunately, that has happened a number of times in the industry," I said. "Trust can become a difficult issue."

"It's not just in the entertainment industry," said Justin. "I know several pastors who've had their moments. In some bigger churches, it has become an issue, unfortunately."

"I guess I never thought that would happen," I said.

"Unfortunately, Staci's response to the issue made things worse," said Justin. "From what you describe here, she seems to have some pride and a little arrogance at work."

"She has told some that she doesn't care what the masses think," I said. "Of course, if you listened to the masses, you would have to take a side or no side at all."

"In my life, I have only one side that I can side with," said Justin. "He reminds me every time when I read and hear His Word."

Celeste said, "Which is good to know."

"I'm a pastor," said Justin, "Staci is an actor. She has taken a side on many things. I have seen her on TV and some of the news items. Some of them are biblically sound. Unfortunately, she has made a few comments here and there that have raised questions and other issues that get into that gray area."

"That's why I went back to see what was being said," I said.

"Have you talked to Staci since this whole thing broke?" asked Justin.

"We saw Staci in Southern California during Christmas," said Celeste. "We have texted some."

I said, "Celeste and I—with the kids— stayed in a condo that Celeste and Staci obtained prior to the first season taping."

"Did she say anything or let on what was going on?" asked Justin.

"She is a professional," I said. "She knows when to not talk shop, especially on an ongoing project. If you give away too many secrets, spoilers can make their way to the public. Who wants to see a story if everyone knows the ending?"

"My heart was troubled during that time," said Celeste. "That was so hard to withhold that from Mike."

Justin asked Celeste, "You didn't tell Mike what was going on?"

"I told her to do that," I said. "She honored my word."

"I think both of you have learned a lot from this experience," said Justin.

"It has caused some trouble at home," I admitted.

Celeste said, "Our kids found out about the show's content."

"All three of them recited a bunch of curse words from the show," I said. "We dealt with it."

"Where did they see the show?" asked Justin.

"Recently, at a neighbor's house," I said. "The kids didn't tell us that was going to happen. We've come to terms with it. Our neighbors didn't mean to show the kids the show."

"They hadn't read the news articles about it," admitted Celeste.

"I visited Focus on the Family's Web site for their review," I said. "They were shocked by the claims of this being marketed as 'family-oriented,' 'family-friendly,' with a 'TV-G' rating."

"Our neighbors know us. They thought Staci and I being strong Christians was a good reason to watch the program," said Celeste.

"That's also troubling. A mislabeled rating," said Justin, "starring some people who've been known to stand for Christian values and family values."

"The questions are being raised as to what 'family values' are being presented," I said.

Justin said, "I'm glad to know that both of you recognize the issue, and both of you are genuinely sorry that this whole misunderstanding has happened."

"I'm not sure if Staci understands," I warned. "Some of the articles that I read—and of course, I don't accept with face value—anything a media outlet will say. The media on more than one occasion have had a tendency to twist and sensationalize."

"If you feel that you need to clear the air, you and Celeste could come before the church body and share your testimony," said Justin.

"I'm not sure I can," said Celeste. "I'm under a contract."

"We plan to get our attorneys involved to go through Celeste's contract," I assured.

"It just hit me," said Celeste, "I'm to the point that I don't want to return for the third season. The show changed so much—with Terrence Forrester and Marian Deavers being dropped and all of this trash added—I don't feel that I can return."

"I'm not inclined to return for any episode," I said. "They trashed my character off camera. It's a real mess until we can get our attorneys involved and negotiate a way to release Celeste to say something before the show ends."

"We can discuss further later. Let's just note that we don't have to make that decision today," said Justin. "We can agree that you and Celeste are willing to come forward to clear your reputations after clearing the legal issues."

"I don't want to cause any trouble for Celeste and Staci," I said. "I didn't know anything about the show's content until a friend passing through town alerted me. I'd been too busy to watch TV."

"The show is being seen by various people," said Justin. "Fortunately, there aren't that many people watching it as if it were on broadcast TV."

"That's true. I had to really search for articles to see anyone really talking about the show," I said. "If it had been on our old network, many more people probably would've been talking about it by now."

"We appeared on a few morning news shows," admitted Celeste.

"How many people do you think really saw those interviews?" I said. "Not as many as in the old days."

"With the content issues that have been described, your old network might have passed on the show," said Justin.

"They did," said Celeste. "They weren't interested...fortunately."

"Ratings are the driving force. Viewers will tune in or not," I said. "If they don't for a returning show, that show is in trouble. Some shows fail to make an entire season sometimes for various reasons."

Justin began, "It'll be interesting to see the outcome of first-season versus second-season numbers. If there's a big drop..."

"A big drop would be a potential death sentence if it were on broadcast TV," I said.

"But this is on a subscription service," said Celeste.

"Which is very different," I said. "No outside advertisers for upset viewers to complain or protest to."

"They may have more accurate numbers than the sample broadcast network ratings," said Justin.

"I don't know if FibreTainment releases such numbers," I said.

Justin said, "Anyway, you may want to see if you can talk with Staci."

"I'll call her," I said.

Justin's cell phone started buzzing.

"I just received a text message from Pastor Mitford," said Justin while looking at his phone. "We have a new issue."

"Now what?" I asked.

Justin continued, "A frat party in Tennessee attempted to recreate a party scene on the TV show."

"I saw that story on InterCable News earlier today," I said.

"I'll tell you, Justin," said Celeste, "that was one of the most irresponsible storylines I've ever seen."

"Did you participate in it?" asked Justin.

"Unfortunately, yes," admitted Celeste, "however, there was no alcohol on the set. It was all fake. The aluminum cans and cups were filled with apple juice."

"I haven't watched that episode yet," I said. "I couldn't get past the first one."

Celeste admitted, "I'll just say that it's awful."

"How awful?" asked Justin.

"I'm not going to be surprised," I grumbled, "but I could guess."

"In addition to the wild drinking, there was a crazy dancing routine," groaned Celeste. "At the end of that episode, Debbie—who is my character—brags the previous night was fun...she implied she 'dishonored herself'...twice...how could she have known while being drunk? That doesn't make sense."

"I told you that I had a suspicion what happened," I said. "I'm not surprised with this show."

"Staci playing Robin didn't get that far," continued Celeste. "They implied Robin passed out. One of the sober guys helped her home."

I began to comment, "As I said—"

Celeste interrupted, disgusted, "You don't have to keep reminding me..."

"That's really disturbing to hear that storyline," said Justin. "The message that I've received is that one student who passed out at the party was transferred to Baptist Memorial Hospital in Memphis. She's on machines."

"Justin, I've never seen anything like this," I said, disgusted. "I've seen more disappointment and sadness."

"People sometimes get crazy ideas," said Justin. "They like to imitate what they see sometimes."

"Celeste, was the fictional frat party *that* fun?" I asked.

"Not really," said Celeste. "It wasn't done in one take."

"You may find this unusual," said Justin. "That young lady's mother contacted the church office yesterday and left a message. She wanted to talk with you and Celeste."

"Let me guess," I said, "she saw Celeste's post."

"Social media doesn't stay in Texas," said Justin. "Celeste had posted on social media that Elizabeth, your oldest daughter, was involved in a special church program three weeks ago."

"Celeste wanted to be back in town to see that," I said. "You posted that on your public page?"

"Staci does similar things on her page," said Celeste.

"You have to be careful doing that," said Justin.

"I agree," I said. "I'd suggest that you hide or remove those posts."

"The mother has called and requested a phone call meeting between Celeste and Staci," said Justin.

"Has this been done before?" I asked.

"I'm not aware of one," said Justin. "The mother has been very kind about this. Actually, her church pastor has contacted us, because she became aware that Celeste posted about being here."

"Is this really wise?" I asked. "If we let one person contact us, we might get a long line of requests."

"That depends on how you live your life and do your walk," said Justin. "In this case, this situation has made national news. The daughter is clinging to life."

"It's not much different when we've received requests to visit sick children or meet people for various events," I said.

"She isn't demanding to talk with you. She has asked that we call from our church with a pastor here," said Justin. "On the other end, she and her pastor would be there."

"What would be the point of the pastors being there?" asked Celeste.

"The pastor at each church would be more like witnesses to assure that no wrongdoing happens during the call."

"I see," I said. "Celeste, I can't force you to do this. If I were the one accused, I would rather have that off my conscience."

"I know what you are saying," said Celeste.

"You aren't obligated to do this," said Justin.

"I would prefer to have my conscience cleared," said Celeste. "I don't know if this will affect my contract. If the mother is a fellow believer, I believe she isn't wanting all of this publicity."

"If something happens to this young girl before we do, we have a mother who may be stuck in a stumbling-block situation," I cautioned.

"I've too big of a heart to pass the opportunity to help this mother," said Celeste, "especially a fellow believer."

"Justin, is the mother a believer?" I asked.

"Yes," assured Justin, "longtime believer. Fifty-six years, according to her testimony and her pastor."

"That's a long time," I said. "Concerning the contract, I think there's a way to handle this. I would be willing."

"Yes, please make the arrangements," said Celeste.

"Okay. I'll make the arrangements," said Justin. "Do you think you will be available the next few days?"

"I will clear my calendar for whatever day you want to meet," I said.

"I have no immediate plans," said Celeste. "We can talk with Mike's parents if they need to stay with the kids."

"We'll be in touch," said Justin. "I'll call y'all."

"Thank you for coming by," said Celeste.

"We'll see what we can do," said Justin.

Before leaving, Justin prayed with us for strength and guidance over the next few days. We also prayed for the mother and daughter who were needing the immediate prayers. After concluding the prayer, Justin left for the evening.

The next day, Justin had made contact with the other church. He did some checking with some friends in the Memphis area to determine if the church and pastor were legitimate. Justin called us to see if the next morning at 10:00 a.m. at our main Spring Creek Church would be appropriate.

The next morning, we drove to the Spring Creek main campus in Plano. We made our way to the church office and met with Justin Lockwood.

Justin, Celeste, and I made our way to a small conference room where he had a speakerphone ready.

"The mother has agreed to talk with you," said Justin. "We'll call and see what happens. You'll be talking with the mother. Her pastor will also be with her."

Justin led Celeste and me in a brief prayer before making the call. Then, Justin dialed the number. We heard the phone ringing. A few moments later, we heard the other church answer the phone. Justin requested to speak to the pastor whose name he had received in the request. Justin had contacted the Memphis area ministry alliance to verify the identity and credentials of the pastor in question. Within a few moments, Justin was speaking with the other church's pastor. Then, the conversation began between the victim's mother and us. For privacy reasons, I'll summarize the conversation:

The doctors were unsure if her daughter would survive. The extreme alcohol poisoning had caused complications. Only time would tell.

The family members didn't blame Celeste and the show for the incident. The victim and her friends made the conscious decision to recreate the frat party from the *"Goodwin Circles Around Again"* TV show and participate in the activities.

The mother was wondering what influenced the decision to take a good TV show and trash it up. Celeste and I shared that we didn't have that answer.

Celeste and I shared our condolences of what had transpired. We would pray for the mother's daughter. We asked that Justin be notified if any issues arose. We wanted to know if any changes happened.

The mother was gracious that we were willing to speak with her. Within twenty minutes, the phone call conversation was over. Celeste and I thanked Justin for his assistance. After returning home, I worked on an audiobook that I was reading for a client. Celeste reviewed and answered some of her fan mail.

At approximately 3:30 p.m., I received a text from Justin that he needed to see Celeste and me. It was very urgent, and he didn't want to talk over the phone. I had a sinking feeling what the issue could be. I told Celeste to hope for the best, but Justin's urgency suggested that something might have happened. Unfortunately, I was correct on the latter.

"Hi, Justin," I said after opening the front door.

"Good afternoon, Mike," said Justin. "I assume Celeste is here."

"She's in the living room reading some fan mail letters," I said. "She's trying to respond to some of them."

"Wow. I've always wondered," said Justin. "How can celebrities answer that volume of mail?"

"It gets sorted by the type of request," I said. "Public relation firms help with some of that."

We walked to the living room. I sat down next to Celeste who had been doing her reading and comments how to respond. I offered Justin the comfy lounge chair.

"How are you, Justin?" greeted Celeste.

"I could be better," said Justin.

"You had something to tell us?" I asked.

I could tell that Justin didn't want to relay something to us. He paused to form what he wanted to say.

"You'd asked if anything had changed to let you know," said Justin. "This concerns the young woman in Tennessee."

Justin's face turned somewhat pale. He twitched one time and a tear fell from his cheek. Celeste and I could tell that the news was emotionally distressing. As he was attempting to form words, I became pessimistic.

"Did she die?" I asked calmly.

Justin was trying to hold back the grief.

"Justin," I asked worriedly, "did she die?"

Justin paused and composed himself. "She returned to the Lord shortly after 1:10 p.m. Central Time this afternoon at Baptist Memorial Hospital in Memphis." He paused again. "She was only twenty years old." A couple of tears fell onto Justin's cheeks as he struggled to find his handkerchief.

Both Celeste and I were struck with shock and grief. Celeste grabbed the box of tissues on a nearby table and offered them to us. The doctors had determined that organ failure quickly became an issue. By this morning, the unidentified twenty-year-old female college student was brain dead and was being kept alive by machines. At approximately 12:30 p.m. Central Time, the family made the final decision to remove the life support.

I began sobbing uncontrollably. Celeste pulled closer to me. She hugged me. I just couldn't hold the emotions. She helped to console me. It was so painful to hear this news. Justin watched as I sobbed and commented.

"How could this happen? She was twenty years old, twenty years old!" I exclaimed. "Her whole life ahead of her!"

"She didn't suffer," said Justin. "She wasn't in any pain when she passed."

"I feel the need to do something!" I said as I tried to wipe my tears.

Justin felt that it was best to not attend the funeral in Memphis or the burial just outside of town. Justin prayed with us again before leaving that day. We prayed for the mother and her family.

Three days later, the funeral for this young lady was held at a Memphis-area church. However, the Memphis church streamed the service over the Internet for family and friends unable to attend on site. The service was beautiful and fitting for that precious life—a young believer since age ten. I asked Justin to get the burial location and the address to send a card. We wanted this family to have the opportunity to grieve without any additional spectacle. In the months to come, I would eventually visit the young lady's grave site when I was on business in the Memphis metro area.

7

THE THREAT GETS PERSONAL

◆————————◆————————◆

As the year progressed, there was some talk that FibreTainment might call for the *"Goodwin Circles Around Again"* cast to assemble for a third season. Summer was quickly approaching. Schools would soon be letting out. I called Staci to see how she was doing. She said that her family was doing well. She had been working on a cable network TV movie the last several weeks. She was saddened to learn about the young college student. She hadn't heard any news of kids imitating the show. I told her that it had happened in Texas—especially at our church home here. I decided to wait for a holiday visit to discuss with her in-person that one situation involved her nieces and nephew.

Over the next few days, several churches canceled my speaking engagements. We got our attorneys involved to determine what action we could take to minimize problems and costs. Albert Jacobs, the series' executive producer, learned that we were raising questions about the show content and Celeste's contract. By May, she decided to give her notice to opt out of a third season on the program. I carefully expressed my concerns with the series. A few commentators speculated something was up when I stated that I wouldn't be appearing on the show. Some of the fans correctly assumed that I wasn't happy with the show.

In April, Staci visited a private Christian college to give a talk about her faith and her work in the industry. It was the first time that she had spoken to that school since accepting the *"Goodwin Circles Around Again"* series. I was unable to watch the live-streamed Web cast. However, the school posted the full video online. For the most part, Staci shared her faith well. The last part of her talk raised some red flags in my mind. I made notes to talk with Staci about those concerns. The next series of events would bring us together in Texas.

Jamie Caballero called me from Los Angeles in mid-May. He alerted us that our hired public relations firm for Celeste had received some threatening anonymous letters. The last few letters became progressively more violent. We also learned that Staci's public relations firm had received some similar letters and a few disturbing social media posts as well. As a precaution, Staci and her family flew back to Texas for a few days to see if the heat would let up. This opportunity gave Staci and me a chance to discuss what really happened.

Staci, Kyle, and their kids flew back in a chartered jet late one night, to not alert fans or local media that she was back in town. We didn't need a media circus unleashed at DFW or Love Field. They stayed with Mom and Dad— who were now living in nearby Frisco. I had blocked the last two weeks of May off from work to spend with Celeste and the kids. I really wanted to visit with Staci, Kyle, and her family.

On Tuesday afternoon, we got the kids and drove from our house to Mom and Dad's home. I pondered on what I would ask Staci. She hadn't changed that much in appearance in thirty years. She had kept very fit. She and Kyle were avidly health conscious and physical fitness advocates.

As we entered Mom and Dad's neighborhood, the warm May sun shrouded around us. Summer was knocking early this year. That was one of the things I loved about Texas. Summers could get hot, but they weren't humid hot like the central Gulf Coast. The dry heat didn't bother me. However, there were days—especially in late June and into July—I would trade the Texas dry heat for the Southern Cal Pacific Ocean morning breezes.

When we arrived, I parked in the driveway next to the rental car that Kyle and Staci had driven from the airport. As we made our way in, Mom greeted us at the door. She was so glad to see us. When we reached the covered back deck, I could see Staci and Kyle's kids running around outside on this wonderful day. Staci was in the living room watching the festivities. She'd been reviewing some old photos with Mom. Dad was out on the back deck watching and enjoying the kids running.

I asked Mom if I could visit with Staci. Celeste and Mom left the living room to join Dad.

"How was your trip from SoCal?" I asked.

"Fine," answered Staci. "It was a little tiring coming in so late last night. I felt a little jet lag getting up this morning."

"I know the feeling."

"I've heard that you wanted to visit with me. You wanted to talk about something?"

"Yes, I have," I said.

I stared for a moment, looking at her. I was pondering what to say and how to say it. This was the same sister who helped me accept Christ twenty-five years earlier. Now, I was having to raise questions about her faith.

"What is it?" asked Staci. "Why couldn't you tell me before now?"

"I wanted to talk with you in-person. How's the TV show going?"

"Fine, I guess. We were given two seasons up front, but Celeste should've already told you that."

"Yes, Celeste did," I responded, "and she told me more."

"What about it?"

"Actually, she told me *a lot more*," I stressed, "and several others have told me as well."

"What about it?"

"I had a chance to watch it two months ago."

"Okay," said Staci, "and?"

"I watched with Celeste."

"And? What are you getting at?"

"Mom warned me to watch the show before I let the kids watch it with us."

"Why do you need to watch this show first without the kids? It's a 'family-friendly' show."

"That's why I said that Mom told me to watch it before the kids did."

"What's this all about not letting the kids watch the show?" asked Staci.

I took a breath and got to the business. "It's some of the content in the show."

"Content in the show? What content?"

"Has anyone told you what happened when Celeste and I tried to watch it?"

"No, what da ya mean you 'tried' to watch it?" said Staci with a very puzzled and suspicious look.

I continued and gradually raised my voice, "What I mean is, Celeste and I tried to watch at least the first episode. As we did, I watched her reaction to it. I was taken aback by the crude humor, the profanity...I've never heard either one of you talk like that before—at least none I chose not to remember—"

"Oh, silly, you know better than that," scolded Staci, "That's not me on the screen. Ya know that. I'm playing a character like we did when we were on the original show."

"We didn't use language like that back then," I retorted.

"That was the 1980s and 1990s on broadcast TV."

"You mean over-the-air broadcast TV?"

"Yes, it's a different world out there. It's not the same as when we were kids."

I was perplexed as I watched Staci. I finally had to say it. "Why do I get the feeling that someone has convinced you that this whole situation is 'okay'?"

"As I just said, times have changed," responded Staci, as if the whole situation was acceptable for the modern day.

"I don't think times have changed as much as you're letting on."

"What are you talking about?"

I heard some of the anger I was feeling slip into my voice. "Almost twenty years ago, I saw the writing on the wall. I saw scripts getting grittier, shallower, and darker."

"Television and movies were getting more realistic. Less on fairy tales and more on reality."

"I guess, when all of this so-called 'reality' TV appeared, the industry had to pander to the lowest of the low," I retorted.

"There are many more options out there today. We can get away with more stuff in a streaming program than broadcast TV, but even broadcast TV had pushed those boundaries some."

"And you're okay with it?" I asked.

Staci began, "I don't know what the big deal is. It's a TV show. It's a fictional work of art…"

"Work of 'art'?' You call *'Goodwin Circles Around Again"* a work of art?! Mozart, Beethoven, even Shakespeare…*that* is art. *'Goodwin Circles Around Again'* doesn't compare to that!"

"Are you mad because you couldn't be on the show and had to miss out because you had to do other work…" began Staci.

"I watched that first episode. I heard Celeste's voice on the TV show as I looked at her. She sat there on our living room couch. Her head drooping, her eyes closing. She acted like the show was ripping every decent and loving thing about her from her soul. She looked like her spirit was dying upon every expletive Debbie Goodwin said."

Staci continued to look at me, her expression puzzled and strange. It seemed like she didn't believe me. I guessed she couldn't see how I could've confused the fakeness of a TV show for reality.

"So you hated the show?!" Staci angrily claimed.

"I couldn't stomach watching more than fifteen minutes of it!" I responded. "I couldn't believe what was going on! I had fair warning!"

"Someone let you know before you watched it…"

"Yes, I learned before Celeste confessed. I couldn't believe what the writers did…"

"Again. It's the 21st century. It isn't the same world that we grew up in. Society has changed so much."

"Wait a minute? You do those 'family-friendly' TV movies," I said. "Those have been very popular. Why act in this new show with all of this…trash?"

"Trash?!" exclaimed Staci.

"Yeah, trash! I've never heard you talk like that…what you have Robin saying!" I yelled. "Celeste hasn't used that kind of language around me and the kids…"

Staci looked at me like I was losing it.

"I take that back…you and Celeste may have said something profane to me at least once in private…but not in front of the kids…y'all asked for forgiveness later after y'all did!"

Staci looked away and said, "I tried to stop some of it. Behind the scenes—"

"That's what I heard you say in your so-called 'testimony' that you did for that private college!"

"So you saw that?"

"Why could you not stop 'all of it'?!'" I asked.

"It's not my show…"

"It's your body, mind, soul, and voice…all that God gave you…is being used to promote this twisted worldview as Robin! She's a total mess!"

"She's not real," responded Staci. "She's only a character…"

"Staci, I don't buy that excuse!" I exclaimed. "The world and the devil can try to give all of us that excuse to allow you the freedom to act or simulate debauchery! That doesn't make it right!"

"You're trying to make this a religious issue? It was never advertised as a Christian show or a religious show!"

"It was advertised with a 'TV-G' rating as a family show! Many people looked up to you because your name alone has become associated with 'family-friendly' entertainment!"

"I've no control over the TV rating!" replied Staci.

"You have control over what you tell people about it being a 'family-friendly show!'".

"By today's standards it is!"

"No, Staci, it's not! A 'TV-G' wouldn't and shouldn't be granted if there were multiple profane words or phrases in the show! One graphic sex joke, sexual innuendo, or sexually-suggestive imagery would put it into at least the 'TV-PG' category…or worse!"

"I can only guess they let it ride if it was only one occurrence…"

"There were multiple occurrences in the first fifteen minutes of that first episode!" I angrily retorted.

"There's nothing I can do now! Two seasons are in the can!"

"Probably should be flushed down the can!"

Staci looked really peeved. "All you can say is this insulting stuff like a bunch of other folks have tried to do!"

"A lot of fans were upset when they got a hint something was wrong!"

Staci said, "This is ridiculous!"

"What about your fellow Christian believers?!" I retorted. "How do ya think they feel seeing a Christian believer—or 'so-called' Christian believer—bashing them for raising questions about your choices and behavior?!"

"Some of those folks are just...complete legalistic jerks! They claim to know their Bible and go around judging everyone!"

"Some of them may be! There are others who are legitimately concerned! All that they know is the persona they see on the screen! They don't really know you! Now they're noticing a definite change in your behavior..."

Staci began, "I'm trying some new ideas to see how they work..."

"God hasn't changed! He hasn't changed his standards!" I yelled. "It appears you've lowered yours..."

Staci looked at me in disbelief. "Oh, you're telling me that you're a better Christian than me?!"

"No! I didn't say that! Look, I'm not perfect; and, I don't try to justify doing stuff that I know is wrong!"

Staci just looked at me, shocked.

Staci cares for Elizabeth, Joe, and Carmen. She loves them just like her kids, Amy and Alex. Staci had enough when I said, "MY KIDS came home singing songs and repeating the profanity they saw on the show after visiting my neighbors. They thought their mom and aunt were cool for that and the other stuff on the show!"

"OH...OH...OH..." grumbled Staci. "You think you're so much better and can claim to be such a goody two-shoes?! I know very well that you've had your moments, too! If ya think you're so 'clean cut,' I suggest that you do a search on the Internet! You'd find an example or two that would embarrass you!"

"What do you mean by that?"

Staci picked up her cell phone, made several quick taps, and put her phone down. My cell phone chimed a text message. Staci had sent a group text to Celeste and my family, her and Kyle's family, and Mom and Dad. I looked at the message. Staci had included a TubeVideo link with the label "Mike Whitman is a TOTAL (**EXPLETIVE**)!!!"

The video had been uploaded a year ago. The description said that video was much older. It looked like someone had used a cell phone camera to record it. As I played the clip, it became apparent someone had recorded me at a motivational speaking meeting. As I watched, I was trying to determine when this was recorded. Obviously, I recognized my slightly younger self in the video talking. From what I could tell, I had concluded my talk. This was the after-the-meeting visit and informal Q&A. I could see that I was trying to get my stuff together. The camera kept staying somewhat out of my sight with some distorted audio.

Another person came up to me and asked, "What are your views on abortion?"

"I've already stated that opinion numerous times," my younger self responded in the recording.

"I was just trying to make sure that you haven't changed your mind."

"I haven't changed my mind. I am tired…and hungry. I've had a long day," I said in the recording. "I'd like to get some dinner so I can unwind."

"So what is your opinion?" haggled the off-camera voice.

"It hasn't changed."

"We just want to know if you're still on the right-to-life side. Only an idiot would take that stance!"

"Oh? If you think adoption is a bad thing...only a (stupid)[2] (jerk) would say that!"

"Wow! And you call yourself a Christian?!"

"Yeah! And if you do not back off, I'll tie your (parts) around your (neck) and you'll then have to consider adoption as your only option! You (jerk)!" The video ended.

"How da ya like that?" scoffed Staci. "I think the kids could easily understand what you said."

"Staci, how could you?!"

"As I said, you aren't so good after all!"

"We aren't done! We're going to have a talk with Mom and Dad! This is a completely unacceptable and an unbiblical way to deal with this matter!"

Staci left the room and went outside. I quickly walked to the covered back deck to let Celeste, Mom, and Dad know what happened.

"Celeste, have you looked at your phone?" I asked.

"No."

"Staci just set everyone here a link to an embarrassing TubeVideo that involves me."

Celeste responded, "She did what?"

"I'm trying to remember where this happened," I said "It looks like me. I got mad at someone about abortion a few years back after a speaking event. Apparently, someone with a cell phone took a video and managed to record me saying some not-so-flattering things toward one of the conference participants, who stuck around afterward trying to mock me. Staci shared that!"

Mom said, "Oh no!"

"Yes, she did!" I said. "Mom, Dad, we need to talk with Staci."

---

[2] Original curse words with more polite equivalence.

Celeste added, "Mike, Staci's posting that text message with your embarrassing video was similar to a plotline in one of the season two episodes."

"Really?" I asked.

"Debbie shares with the whole family the video where she found Davey in bed with the older woman," said Celeste.

"Oh, good grief!" said Dad.

"I wanted you to know," said Celeste.

"That show is causing more trouble than it's worth," I said.

A few minutes later, Mom, Dad, Staci, and I were in Mom's and Dad's kitchen sitting around the kitchen table. Staci was sitting across from me. She wasn't happy.

Dad said, "Young lady, I've no idea why you chose to share that video with everyone."

"To prove that Mike is a goody-goody two-shoes!" retorted Staci.

"Why do that? For what purpose?" asked Mom.

"There've been people going around claiming *he* is a better Christian than me!" exclaimed Staci.

"Maybe I don't go around and post stuff for people to make a comparison!" I responded.

"Young lady, your mom and I helped to bring both of you into this world. We tried to raise you right," said Dad.

"It doesn't make sense why you shared that video," said Mom.

"She got the idea to embarrass me from the TV show," I answered. "I can explain the video."

Dad said, "Please explain."

I continued, "The video is at least eight years old. I was talking in either Omaha or Kansas City, I can't remember where. I had an individual try to provoke me about my views on abortion. That individual got me mad. I was hungry and tired at the end of my presentation. I wanted to go back to my hotel room to get refreshed and a bite to eat. That was it!"

Dad scolded, "You shouldn't have used that kind of language."

I began, "I understand and agree with that—"

Dad stared at me. I had forgotten to say something that I had to say when I got into trouble with him. I may have been a major child star back in the day. I was still a kid. I was *his* kid.

"I understand and agree with you, *sir*."

"You have to be very careful," said Dad, "I've told you many times you never know if someone is going to have a camera recording."

"We taught you that could happen with possible recordings. You never know if a microphone is live," reminded Mom.

"Unlike those days when I could discipline you, you're fully grown," said Dad. "You'll have to decide what to do about this situation. I'd recommend that you repent to those who saw it. If you can ever contact those people in the video..."

"Dad, the video doesn't show where I apologized," I said. "After I got back to my hotel that night, I contacted my client. I apologized. They tried to locate the conference participant, who they found wouldn't accept my apology."

"You'll have to be very careful," cautioned Dad.

"Which now leads to this issue about Staci," I said.

"Young lady, you know better than to cause this trouble among our family," warned Dad. "Did you know the full story behind Michael's encounter?"

"No, sir," said Staci, "I didn't." She lowered her head.

"Michael and Celeste believe they know why you may have chosen to do this," said Mom.

"My TV show," answered Staci.

"Yes, this TV show," said Dad. "'Goodwin Spins Around and Around Again'... whatever it is."

"It isn't exactly my TV show," said Staci. "I don't have full creative control."

"I understand that," said Dad. "Unfortunately, the situation is much more complicated than it was nearly thirty years ago."

"We didn't want to admit it. I've watched some of the episodes," said Mom. "We had received word from other friends when they saw it. Your dad has a very sensitive heart...his spiritual heart, where he couldn't take a chance watching the program."

"Staci, I love you for who you really are," said Dad. "To watch a program where you portray someone so drastically different can be heartbreaking to watch."

Staci lifted her head.

"Do you remember that movie where you played a sadistic murderer?" asked Dad.

"That's a long time ago." Staci lowered her head again.

"You may remember how I felt when I watched it?" asked Dad. "Without any warning?"

"Yes, sir," Staci answered.

"I remember that one a little too well," I said. "The critics blasted the performance."

"Staci, you tried to deny any of the criticism." Mom gave her a look.

Dad resumed, "It was a role that you had trouble pulling off convincingly."

"And all of the fake blood didn't help either," Staci agreed. "Some of the fans back then were appalled."

"From what I recall, some people wanted to laugh through some of the scenes because it looked so silly." I wasn't smiling.

"That's one role that I had to try burying for the next decade." Staci cringed.

"Unfortunately, it resurfaces from time to time on late-night movie schedules"—

I winced—"especially at Halloween."

"You may recall what happened." Mom looked around at us and then back at Staci.

"Actually, it was years later," said Staci. "That's one reason why I took time away from acting."

"Have Amy and Alex seen *'Goodwin Circles Around Again'*?" I asked.

"They don't want to watch it. Kyle doesn't either," said Staci. "He's had a problem with many of my projects. He'll step out of the room when some of the romantic kissing scenes happen with my male co-stars. Those scenes aren't over the top, but it still bothers him."

"I'm not surprised," I answered. "Celeste and I have an agreement about kissing other people. We don't kiss other people outside of our marriage."

"This new show is too much for your dad to watch," said Mom. "I've watched a certain amount of it. The role of Robin no longer fits who you are. Years ago, you were able to play the part well. This updated version of the character is too...difficult to watch. You've outgrown the role...not only physically but spiritually."

"It never was me even back in the eighties and nineties on the original show."

"True," agreed Mom. "However, you've changed a lot since 1988, and even more in the last ten years."

"Off camera, I've watched two young kids grow up to accept the Lord," said Dad. "Those kids also helped your mom and me to know Him better and accept Him. I will always be grateful. I am also very grateful that we met Terrence Forrester. He and his family helped us with God during those early years."

"They helped me overcome the hurtful and judgmental feelings I had toward church, my view of God, and my relationship with Christ," Mom sighed.

"Christianity isn't a religion. It's far more than that," said Dad. "It's a way of viewing life now and the life to come. It gives our present life a purpose to live. Staci, I'm concerned that this program and some of its trappings is causing you to drift away from what you encouraged us to believe so many years ago."

"As I've told Mike, it's nothing more than a TV show," Staci piped up.

"Actually, there's more going on there than a TV show." Mom gave her a look. "There's a worldview being presented that contradicts your own beliefs...your Christian beliefs."

"After watching your testimony at that college, I noticed that you said some things that seemed to compromise your faith. I could be mistaken." Dad's voice was firm. "You said something about only getting some of the content removed despite the jokes that did make it to the air. You didn't really address that. While you may have won some of the battles to remove some of the content to glorify God, Satan was able to win those other battles where other sinful items remained. In those losses, Satan's agenda was glorified instead. In other words, a little leaven remained to ruin the whole batch—remember Galatians 5:9. Although *'Goodwin Circle'* and this new show were not Christian or religious programs, the latter has more than its fair share of leaven to diminish the whole point of having the show and for you to even be associated with the project. All of Galatians 5 would be a good passage for you to review."

"It was a very busy morning. I may've said it wrong." Staci looked chagrined. "I was somewhat out of sorts that day, sir."

"Luke 10:27 is another Scripture passage that comes to mind," Mom added.

"Look, I can't stay in here right now," complained Staci. "I need some time to think."

Staci ran out of the kitchen. She seemed a little flustered and distraught. Mom and Dad were showing her where her choices had sometimes had consequences, including how it had affected our family over the years.

"Apparently, we must have struck a chord with her," Dad sighed.

"Or at her conscience," I agreed. "She can't deny when her parents are being faithful."

"You noticed that." Mom smiled slightly.

"Of course." I smiled.

"I'm not sure what else we can do at this point. She's a grown woman." Dad looked thoughtful. "It's not like I can discipline her like a child."

"There's only one other person outside of us and Christ, who might be able to do anything," Mom said.

Dad and I looked at Mom with anticipation wondering who she was going to suggest. Then Mom said, "Kyle."

"Yes," I agreed. "Kyle, her husband. I have an idea." I got up from the table. "We'll see what God and Kyle can do."

I walked back into the living room. All of the kids were playing. Celeste was helping watch the kids.

"Celeste, did you see where Staci went?" I asked.

"I think I saw her walking toward her room." Celeste glanced at me. "She said she felt a little tired."

"The conversation got a little heated, but Staci is determined to stay focused on that TV show," I explained.

"Isn't that something!" Celeste frowned.

"Have you seen Kyle?" I asked.

"The last I saw him, I think he was reading a newspaper on the back porch."

Celeste stayed with the kids, who were having a lot of fun. As I walked back to the covered porch, I approached Kyle.

"Reading up on the news?" I asked.

"There's a lot happening in north Texas," said Kyle.

"I thought you might like a break away from the house. Would ya like to get out for a little bit?"

"Whatcha have in mind?" asked Kyle.

"There's a sports bar in the country club. We don't have to stay there long. They have several TV screens with ballgames on and maybe some other sports. I'd also like to visit with you."

I knew Kyle liked various sporting events. He agreed that we could get away from the house for a few minutes. I told Celeste, Mom, and Dad where we were going. We would be back before supper. My parents' gated community had an eighteen-hole golf course connected to it. The sports bar was a really nice touch. I don't like to drink alcohol. When I usually visit, I stay away from those drinks. While I don't have a problem with someone choosing to drink alcohol; I have a problem with it if they do it to excess and get drunk.

We walked into the bar. Along one wall, several flat-screen TVs were showing a wide variety of baseball games, sporting events, and a couple of ordinary entertainment shows. It was not always wall-to-wall sports. We took seats near the TVs and I ordered a soft drink. Kyle chose the same. Supper was in three hours, so we didn't want to spoil our appetites.

I noted the TV screens. "I see the local teams are playing."

"Have you been keeping up with them?"

"Not closely."

"You didn't have me come down here just to talk sports, did you?"

"No," I said, "I actually have a much bigger concern. Has Staci said much about her involvement in this new TV show?"

"Only a little. I let her do her acting projects. She's a grown woman."

"Have you watched the show?"

"No," said Kyle. "It's one of those boundaries."

"Why?"

"It's not her in those shows."

"When she starred in *'Goodwin Circle,'*" I said, "she was playing a role that was not her."

"Actually, I will watch that show, and of course, its two TV movies that I acted with…y'all," said Kyle, attempting the southern talk.

"Really? Why?"

Kyle paused and then said, "Because it's one of those few shows where she's most like herself. I get to see her grow up from a girl to a young woman. The whole innocence is what I see."

"I can assure you she and I had a few arguments and off-camera fights; and unfortunately, I helped to cause a few."

Kyle laughed. "Part of growing up. I've watched Amy and Alex do the same thing."

"One concern I have is the negative impacts that this TV show has had on some fellow believers."

Kyle looked puzzled. "Ok? Tell me more."

"You saw the video clip she sent earlier?"

"I've seen it before."

"That video was taken out of context. I sought forgiveness from the event sponsor and the conference participant who was involved with the recording," I said. "The sponsor accepted. The participant refused. Then, that video surfaced on the Web recently."

"There are always two sides to everyone's story. I appreciate you telling me what happened."

"I plan to discuss when we gather tonight as a family, to ask for forgiveness what was shown in that video."

Kyle said, "I commend you for doing that."

"I don't know if Staci will want to ask for forgiveness for what she did. Celeste and I are wondering if the TV show is affecting Staci's behavior and choices in some way."

"I've heard some actors accidentally pick up unexpected traits. I've addressed some of that with Staci. She's tried to address them if I notice them."

"In a season two storyline that is expected to release later this year, Staci's character is involved in sharing an embarrassing online item with several family members; and it becomes the foundation for several crude jokes and sexual innuendos toward Davey Goodwin."

"That's unfortunate…and especially toward your character on the show."

"Yep. This TV show has had a negative impact on countless fans of hers…and ours. Have you kept up with any of it?"

"I've seen a few items in the news. You might have to enlighten me a little what you've seen."

"Is Staci still a believer?" I asked. "A Christian?"

"To my knowledge she still is."

"Some of her behavior is an attempt to justify the worldview being presented on this new TV show. The mainstream news isn't covering the negative impact this show has had on various believers. Some of the lesser-read media have revealed that several believers have been hurt emotionally…and spiritually."

"She can't please everyone. They shouldn't be putting her on a pedestal…she's only human. She's had some stress since taking that project."

"Are you there to see what has been happening?" I asked.

"I've had to set my boundaries," said Kyle, "have you?"

"Has Staci tried to set any boundaries?"

"She has some. She's told me she's had to get the production staff to rethink some scenes, some content, and some other items. She doesn't have full creative control. She's wanted to try some new directions."

"Those new directions are getting her in hot water. Many Christian believers have been upset because they felt they were deceived. They were given the impression that the show would be 'family-friendly' because of the 'TV-G' rating, Staci's name being associated with the project because of her past 'family-friendly' choices, and the implied promotions that Staci and Celeste made on talk and news shows prior to the premiere."

"I see."

"For a Christian like her to accept doing the things that she's accepted to do, it's caused some spiritual damage to...only God knows how many...who were expecting her to uphold her values. One college student is dead in Tennessee because the show inspired a crazy event that turned tragic in real life. It's impacted some of the children's ministries at our church here in Plano. Kids were reciting negative catchphrases and songs with profane words from the show. Even my kids watched the show at the neighbor's one night. They ended up repeating curse words because they saw Aunt Staci and their mom parroting their characters' lines. When I learned about the show's content, I couldn't believe what I was watching."

"Now that you mention it, I've had a few close friends tell me about it," said Kyle. "I didn't want to admit. Some think it's funny that Staci is doing it. I understand where you're coming from."

"When I tried to watch the show with Celeste, I felt the Holy Spirit grieving. I looked at Celeste. She seemed like she was reliving the whole experience. I was told she cried in the car with Staci every day. I had also heard Staci even cried during some lunch breaks in her dressing room."

"Staci wasn't always crying about the show. She really felt for Celeste. She knew Celeste wasn't happy. Staci was missing me during those lunch breaks."

"Staci may be strong enough to endure the craziness. The crude humor and some of the edgy imagery is creating too much confusion and dissonance. It's just a matter of time until she cracks under the strain, or some of her fans do."

"I understand what you're saying," said Kyle. "If you continue to grieve the Holy Spirit by insulting Him, you'll eventually have trouble hearing Him—therefore, quenching the Spirit *[Ephesians 4:30, 1 Thessalonians 5:19, Hebrews 10:29, Hebrews 3:7-11]*."

"Yes, if one gets that far gone, they fall away like an unbeliever *[1 Timothy 4:1-3]*," I said. "They may continue to play an act of being a believer—going to church, reading the Bible, praying, etc., but the Word has little impact on their life choices *[2 Timothy 3:1-17, 1 Corinthians 5:11-13, James 4 especially James 4:17]*."

"That's some very powerful stuff there...now that you've shared with me what has been going on."

"Celeste and I have lawyers examining her contract to see what we can do. Celeste is planning to leave the show after season two is released."

"I plan to have a talk with Staci about all of this. She has been good to follow my requests," said Kyle. "She respects me...and loves me. She's often told folks that she looks to me for that spiritual guidance within our marriage."

"Celeste has been understanding with me as well. Staci may not realize all of the issues that are at stake. With her being the leading star, I can understand feeling the pressure to succeed; wanting to be with friends; and attempting to bring an updated slant to a classic show. Unfortunately, this show is nowhere near the quality that *"Goodwin Circle"* was. Her participation in the ungodly language, behavior, and scenes—regardless if it was simulated—doesn't give her a license to do it as a Christian *[1 John 3:6-9, Romans 6:1-2, Romans 6:15-23]*."

"You're right about that. I'll talk with her," said Kyle. "In fact, I'll get the Word and share with her several passages that she needs, to understand why she may want to rethink doing this project or others like them."

"We are Christians! We're to be *in* the world, not *of* the world *[John 17:14-16]*. Whatever we choose to do, we must do it for the Glory of God *[1 Corinthians 10:31]*. Anything that is not reflective of His nature in our lives, those things aren't from Him *[1 John 2:16]*. Needlessly hurting other Christians for personal gain should never be considered in the heart of a true believer *[Matthew 6:1-34, Philippians 2:3, James 3:16, 1 Corinthians 10:24]*."

After Kyle and I finished our individual drinks, I paid the bill. Staci had taken some controversy a few years back when asked if she agreed with Ephesians 5:25. While she said yes, there were some in the masses that were taken aback by her comments. Then again, Staci and I didn't write the Bible. God inspired many to compose its many pages ages ago.

We returned to Mom and Dad's home. Mom had ordered a special dinner. However, she included a few homemade side dishes that some of us hadn't had for a while. Later that evening, I would get the chance to share with the family how I felt about Staci's betrayal of trust.

8

REDEMPTION

◆━━━━━━◆━━━━━━◆

After Kyle and I returned to Mom and Dad's home, Kyle and Staci went outside to the backyard and sat in the covered freestanding porch swing. Mom and Dad didn't have many shade trees at their home. This swing made it easier for them, especially in the hot Texas summers.

As I looked out to the backyard, I could see that Kyle was talking with Staci. For some reason, I felt that God was reassuring me that Kyle would be able to get through to her. Kyle was using God's Word to speak to Staci, that her pride and arrogance wasn't the way to handle any situation, including this.

Kyle told me later that he had searched for a list of Bible verses. As he talked with Staci, God spoke through Kyle.[3]

Kyle said he shared the passage of Ephesians 5:22-23 about wives honoring their husbands. He asked Staci to make amends with the family, with friends, and, if possible her fans. He also asked that she be more careful next time when taking acting roles, by making sure that she didn't put

---

[3] These passages can be found in an appendix at the end of this book.

herself in a similar situation as she did with the new show's contract. He asked her to reconsider her willingness to kiss her co-stars in her projects unless he was the one involved. Staci turned and reached to hug him. I was told later that she had shed a couple of tears. Her heart had become broken and contrite. After hugging, they both took a moment to pray to repent to God and her rededication to Christ.

Mom announced that dinner was ready. We were in for a special Texas barbecue meal that Mom and Dad had ordered. It had been a while since I had barbecue. It was always a treat to have when at home in Texas.

When Staci and Kyle walked in from outside, Staci appeared to whisper to Dad about something. Dad walked over to me and told me that Kyle had used God's Word to help Staci understand what needed to change. With God's help, we would also need to find a way to help our family, our friends, and our different fan bases heal from all of the strife, calamities, and negativity *"Goodwin Circles Around Again"* had wrought. Following dinner, our families gathered for a special family meeting. It had been years since all of us were together in the same room in this way.

"Alright, everyone, we have some important things to share with y'all," said Dad. "I ask that y'all listen closely. Mike?"

"Ok, everyone," I began, "we need to share some things as a family. Before we address anything involving *'Goodwin Circles Around Again,'* I have one personal item."

I paused and continued, "As many of you know, Staci texted to y'all a link to a video clip that someone had uploaded to TubeVideo. This video appears to be me after one of my motivational talks several years ago—about nine years ago I think, in Kansas City. It appears that I got into a very heated discussion—to put it mildly. It was late in the day. I'd just finished. As the audience dispersed, someone approached me to get into a confrontation about my views on abortion. I was tired, I was hungry, and I wasn't wanting to stay for a long argument on that issue. One thing led to another. I lost my cool. The man wouldn't stop. I uttered a few...'words'...then security had to get involved to remove that man. It wasn't fun. I didn't know at the time someone was nearby recording with a video camera. I haven't seen this video until now."

"Unfortunately, I don't remember all of the details of that day. When I saw the video, that part of that day came back. It was me. I lost my cool for a brief moment. My emotions took ahold of me—I let my anger get the best of me. All that I can say is, 'I have to own up to it. It was me.' I ask that you forgive me for using that language and treating those individuals that way on that evening, despite the other circumstances that happened."

After everyone expressed that they were willing to forgive me. I continued, "I don't know if there are other videos out there. I can't remember all of the talks that I've done. Did I act like this elsewhere? I don't remember. If for some reason other examples should surface, I ask that you also forgive me for that. I know many times I've asked the Lord in private later when I messed up."

"Mike, Did you tell me that you were going to do something else?" asked Celeste.

"Oh, yes. Although I probably shouldn't have to do it, I'm volunteering to take two weeks of no Internet because of this."

Mom began, "Mike, you don't have to do that..."

"I'm insisting, Mom," I said. "I let the kids down. I let Celeste down...I let many people down."

"What are you going to do with your time?" asked Dad. "You do some of your work over the Internet."

"That's true, Dad," I answered. "The exception will be to do my work. No casual browsing or fun stuff. Only business."

"Don't you read a Bible online?" asked Dad.

"I don't need the Internet to read the Bible," I answered.

The family laughed, and I knew Dad was kidding around.

"I'll make sure that he sticks to his leisure Internet ban because I have a few things that he can use that extra time to get done," quipped Celeste.

"It's really a 'Honey-Do' list," I remarked. "Honey do this, and honey do that."

"Actually, I've updated this list," answered Celeste. "I could use some help."

Everyone laughed when I looked surprised. Of course, I was playing along with her, but I was serious about my two-week Internet ban.

After everyone quieted down, Celeste began, "Now that Mike has shared with you his confession. I've two things to share."

"First, most of you have probably learned by now that Staci and I were involved in reviving our former roles of our old TV series 'Goodwin Circle.' The new show is on FibreTainment. This experience has been very difficult for me. Staci and I spent many weeks in the studio last fall and earlier this spring to get episodes taped. Mike's aware of some of the difficult aspects of the show. When Mike learned about the show's direction, he wasn't happy."

Celeste continued, "If I could change anything, I should've been stronger to say 'no' to what they wanted to do. It would've been better for them to just fire me than to compromise what I truly believe. A TV show is a fleeting thing. Family is a much stronger reason to live, and Christ is one whom I should be giving the glory."

Celeste turned to the kids. "Kids, I feel that I've helped create a stumbling block for you and others. My character's behavior on the new show is something that I'm not proud of. I fought to get content removed...yes, there was content that didn't make it to the final draft. What made it to the final show is still wrong. I know that for some of you kids that may be difficult for you to understand. I don't want to watch it not only because I believe the content is inappropriate, but also, I'm embarrassed that I convinced myself to do some of the scenes. We never attempted to do on our old show what we did on this new show."

I said, "Unfortunately, I didn't allow her to tell me anything about the plotlines. I'll never let that happen again because she felt guilty for doing some of this stuff, despite honoring her word and my request. She really wanted to tell me during our California visit last Christmas. I'm sorry you had to go through that."

"There's one first season episode that was really awful," said Celeste. "I'm truly embarrassed now that I did it. It inspired a real college fraternity in Tennessee to recreate a scene from that episode. The real-life consequences were tragic. I've yet to even watch the episode myself; I just can't. At this time, that's the only tragic event that we know about that this new show has caused."

"We don't know if any other college students have attempted the stunts that were portrayed." I added, "If it happened and didn't make the national news, we may never know."

Celeste continued, "To all of you, I ask for your forgiveness: for my portrayal of Debbie Goodwin on the show; for compromising my own values of good taste and morality when the writers gave Debbie inappropriate language to say and actions to do…I should've refused; and, for the emotional, mental, and spiritual fallout this TV show has inflicted on many. I love all of you far too much to let this TV show become any stumbling block for you and your faith. At many times over the last few months, I've asked Christ to help me through those days when I felt that I couldn't take another moment. My faith in Christ has protected me. I've asked Him to forgive me. Therefore, I humbly ask…*all of you*…to forgive me." With that, Celeste shed a few tears.

"Wow! I'm surprised that you endured all of that," answered Amy, my niece.

"It makes me want to know what else Aunt Celeste and Mom did to cause all of this," said Alex, my nephew. "Mom didn't let on. I didn't want to watch to find out."

"If I hadn't had Christ there, I don't know—," Celeste trailed off.

"Unfortunately, I wasn't the best emotional support during those days. I tried to understand what she was going through," admitted Staci. "I tried to cope with it, but I often tried to deny it."

"When we left work each evening, we didn't discuss work unless we had a scene we needed to practice or recite," Celeste continued. "Those days that we didn't have to practice scripts or memorize lines…"

Staci interjected, "We set boundaries about the work…"

Celeste continued through her tears, "Again, I ask for your forgiveness what I did; and, if you ever watch this show someday, please forgive me…"

Our family agreed to forgive Celeste. Finally, Staci stepped forward to express her feelings and her confession—shedding tears at various times throughout.

"That now leaves me," began Staci. "I've done quite a bit to cause a lot of emotional issues for many. When I saw the contract for '*Goodwin Circles Around Again*,' I was under the impression that the show was going to be a continuation of the old show. Celeste was also under that same impression. When we recorded our first pilot episode…yes, there were two pilots. That first pilot had a much different vibe…a positive vibe…that the eventual show didn't have. Unfortunately, the test audience didn't respond favorably to it…at least, that is what Celeste, the other cast members, and I were told. The writers and the executive producer had a meeting shortly after they learned about the first pilot's results."

"We had some people quit and some new writers hired. Some of those new writers weren't willing to change a script. Some were very determined that the show would have the dark and gritty vibe that the second test audience claimed the first pilot lacked. The executive producer encouraged the grittier stuff. At the time, I thought I might be able to negotiate removing the material. Those writers would only compromise to a certain extent. The second test audience enjoyed it. The studio believed the results. This is why the second pilot led to the 'green lighting' of the series. From what I've learned, the first season received a lot of views on FibreTainment. I knew that all of the crazy stuff was bothering Celeste: the bizarre clothing choices, the excessive adult language, the alcohol usage, and drunken behavior. Kids, we weren't really drunk."

Staci paused and then continued, "To Mike's kids, you unfortunately saw the show. Your mom and dad told me that the three of you had visited a neighbor one night and watched a few episodes of the new show. Some of the phrases and songs that you repeated had some awful content. I'm very sorry that I helped in exposing you to that. I know your mom has asked for her forgiveness already for what she did and what we allowed our characters to do in the show."

"I've been involved in show business since I was six years old. I took some time away to have two wonderful kids—Amy and Alex. I love all of you—including Elizabeth, Joe, and Carmen. I love being with all of you. I'd never want anything to hurt you. I certainly wouldn't want any role that I portrayed to cause you any harm…especially any spiritual harm."

"Earlier this afternoon, I had some discussions with Mom, Dad, and Mike about the new show and the text message that I sent. Kyle and I also spent some time late this afternoon until dinnertime discussing what we should do. This TV show has had varying effects on you...our fellow believers in Texas, California...and around the country and the world. As Mike mentioned, we have one unfortunate consequence—one college student's death and many others in lesser but difficult consequences in Tennessee...that's all that's known so far. There could be others out there and elsewhere."

"Kyle and I talked. He shared several Bible passages with me," continued Staci, "When he reminded me...as a Christian, if my actions and words could result in one of God's children to stumble—to fall from their faith in Christ—God stirred in my heart. I also thought that my personal material gains of money, things, and influence of this world fell tremendously short of Christ's salvation for my fellow believers. If I should cause a fellow believer who isn't strong in Christ to fall away...to sin...or to deny Christ, God would hold me accountable. My Christian faith and walk would be completely damaged if I continued on the path that...unfortunately...I've been on. Kyle shared many Scriptures with me. After discussing with him, we decided that I...that we...would need to make some serious changes."

"I realize now that while *'Goodwin Circles Around Again'* is make-believe, my participation in the recent storylines and the behavior portrayed is a complete contradiction to my personal and Christian values. While I've tried to deny that the whole show is nothing but make-believe and me portraying someone else, I now realize that my testimony and walk was much stronger prior to taking on this new project. Celeste has expressed to me that she is pondering the decision to leave the show after season two. We've yet to know if there'll be a season three. I thought I could argue out much of the bad stuff from the storylines...I failed! While God was glorified in the battles that I was able to win, Satan jumped for glee on those battles I lost...the stuff that made it to the finished show. As a result, a very imperfect show with an imperfect cast tried to play imperfect people. Instead of God truly being glorified, God was mocked at the same time while Satan enjoyed—with millions of others—watched me make a total fool of myself. God made sure that He'd be glorified by turning my fellow true believers away and not accepting the content that I was being asked to portray or pretend. All of those scenes that you saw alcohol, were staged. There wasn't any alcohol there; fruit juice was used instead. All of the drunken behavior was really bad overacting."

"This show has weakened my faith by affecting me and some of my fellow believers. I matured greatly in the faith during the 2000s while I was away from Hollywood. I learned more in God's Word that I wasn't aware when I first accepted Christ back in 1993. When I accepted Christ, I wasn't alone that day. Mike was there with me that one afternoon after a day at the studio when we stopped for a snack. It was that afternoon that Mike and I first accepted and dedicated our lives to Christ."

"I ask that you forgive me for getting involved in this project, for letting the writers take advantage of me to cave my family values and God's values—that I've believed for a long time. For not having a clear head and a clear conscience to realize the potential devastating effect that my parroting of the words and actions in my portrayal of this older...and dumber...Robin Goodwin...would have on those watching this program. I humbly ask for forgiveness. I've tried to stay closer to the Word during this whole time. I now realize I need Christ more than ever at this time."

As we sat there, we could tell that Staci had received a change of heart. God had cracked her heart's veneer. It had melted to reveal a contrite heart in need of Christ's salvation and grace. Staci shed several tears.

"Also, I ask for your forgiveness for sharing that embarrassing nine-year-old video of Mike that I found online from that conference," said Staci. "That was completely inappropriate of me to share that with y'all. I completely violated God's Word. If I'd had a problem with it, I should've called Mike to discuss it in private. I violated Matthew 18 *[Matthew 18:15-35]*. It wasn't proper for me to share. Also, as Mike said, the video was taken out of context. He later asked for forgiveness from the conference sponsor. He attempted to ask forgiveness from the conference participant, yet that second person refused. I should've never inflicted my nieces and nephew with a video like that without talking with Mike. I was very wrong. I also ask for forgiveness for that as well."

We looked at Staci as she cried. To see her there, I felt assured that God was working on her heart, soul, and mind.

"I forgive you, sis," I said. The rest of the family agreed.

"Sis, I feel moved that we need to take this moment while we're here...the three of us...you, Celeste, and I...should take the opportunity to rededicate our lives to Christ before our family," I said. "Everyone, we're merely human like the rest of you. We're sinners like the rest of you. We need the power of Jesus Christ to be in us *[Ephesians 2:13-22]*, to cleanse us of our sins *[1 John 1:9]*, and to have our trust in Him *[Galatians 5:5-6, Ephesians 2:8-9]*. For if our hearts are truly with Him and He is with us, no one not even death can separate us from Him *[Romans 8:37-39]*."

"Yes, I would like to do that," agreed Staci. "Very much like us...all those years ago."

"Staci, there are more of us here now than there were on that day in 1993." I smiled. "How about if we all join hands and pray together? We're family. Why not include them?"

We were all arranged around the room sitting in various places. We all stood up and gathered hands in a circle and bowed our heads to pray.

I began, "Let us pray. Dear Lord, we gather during this family time. We ask that you join us here now as our children and parents/in-laws witness our rededication to Your Son, Jesus Christ. Dear Lord Jesus, I'm a sinner. While I accepted You years ago, I haven't always been as faithful as I should be. Please forgive me of my iniquities; especially those that were revealed to my family. Continue to teach me and encourage me to seek your guidance in all that I do. Please reenter my heart so Your Light will shine and make me new. Thank you for all of the blessings you've bestowed over the years. It's Your Will, not my will. In Your Holy Name I pray."

Celeste prayed, "Dear Lord, I know I've asked many nights and many days over the last several months to forgive me for my participation in this TV show and for the effects that it has had on my children and others. Please forgive me of my pride, arrogance, and self-deceitfulness. I rededicate my life to serving You. Please continue to guide Mike in helping me stay on the straight and narrow path. Continue to show me Your Way, for it's the only True Way. Thank you for all that You've done for our family, our friends, and loyal fans. Please help our fellow believers learn to know that we truly love You and are Yours. Lord Jesus, I ask all of this in Your Name."

Then Staci prayed, "Lord Jesus, I've really made a mess of things. I compromised Your Word on several occasions. I failed to truly uphold Your Biblical standards and Your Word, which You taught me. I let Satan deceive my heart and my mind. I allowed my selfish desires to take hold rather than follow Your Word. I must admit that Mike has been a better Christian these last several months than I have. Of course, I shouldn't be comparing myself to him. He isn't much better than me."

"As you may have noticed Lord, Mike just squeezed my hand acknowledging in agreement." I jokingly squeezed Staci's hand, though there was some laughter among the group.

"In all seriousness, Lord, I rededicate myself to you," continued Staci. "Please forgive me of all of the sins that I committed in the production of this TV show. Please also forgive me for all of the trouble I've inflicted on my fellow believers and fans. I pray for the students and families that were affected by trouble and tragedy back in the spring at the college in Tennessee. I pray for the young Daughter in Christ who lost her life that spring evening. Please continue to comfort her mother and family members to continue their trust in You."

"I'm now aware that many were truly hurt in this situation in many ways. I also helped deceive them in believing I would be in a 'family-friendly' show that was anything but. May all of those who may have received pain and suffering, receive Your comfort. May those whose hearts were hardened by my pride and arrogance, receive Your comfort as well. May those who may have been hurt by my selfishness, brashness, and unmindfulness, receive healing in their hearts and minds. I desire to reconcile with the fans and others who may have been affected. I lay down all of my pride, self-centeredness, arrogance, and other iniquities. I desire to follow You and accept Your call once again. It's through Your grace that You saved us many years ago. It'll be Your grace again that will guide us now and evermore. Thank you. Lord Jesus."

I concluded, "In the name of the Father, the Son, and the Holy Spirit, Amen."

Upon the conclusion of the prayer, I could feel a sense of relief covering the room.

"Staci, do you feel that?" I asked.

"I do."

"Do y'all feel anything different?" I asked the others.

Many of us felt like a change had happened in the room. The mood was of peace, love, joy, kindness, goodness...everything of the Fruit of the Spirit *[Galatians 5:22-23]*.

"That feeling that Staci and I received in 1993," I said.

"It *is* the feeling I remember," said Staci.

I smiled. "The settling of our conscience. Some may view this as God's Presence—the Fruit of the Spirit. Staci and I felt that in 1993. Here again, today. He has always been there. We asked to rededicate our lives and repent."

I retrieved my cell phone and opened my Bible app. I searched for Psalm 9. As I read Psalm 9, I referred to Psalm 9:9-10 *[NASB]*: *"The Lord also will be a stronghold for the oppressed, A stronghold in times of trouble; And those who know Your name will put their trust in You, For You, O Lord, have not forsaken those who seek You."*

For the rest of the evening, we decided to focus on something that was good and wholesome. Mom and Dad had the complete DVD collection of the old *"Goodwin Circle"* TV show. The set included all ten seasons with original pilot, bloopers, various extras, and the two TV movies. I suggested that we watch some of the funny bloopers. I insisted that we watch the doorknob blooper where Celeste's first appearance happened. After all of these years, that one was still very special. While we, as a family, had come to reconcile over the new TV show debacle, the situation was only partially over. We still had attorneys reviewing Celeste's contract. Staci agreed to allow the attorneys to review her contract to see what we could do. We wanted the ability to publicly ask for an apology or request forgiveness without legal ramification. The next few days would bring some positive changes. God was in control. He knew that we weren't happy with Staci and Celeste being stuck in their situation. Season two wouldn't become available for a few more months. The season three renewal was still unknown. The next series of events led to some interesting results.

9

THE BIG NEWS BREAKS

◆ ◆ ◆

I asked everyone to come back and visit our home in Plano two days later. I was really happy to visit with everyone at our home because we had a little more room. Staci and her family arrived around 2:00 p.m. All of the kids were ready to have some fun in the backyard. The four of us parents were going to spend some time together. I had turned on the TV to see if I could find a good movie, a TV show, or something else.

By coincidence, this channel was showing a very familiar movie promo.

"Hey, everyone, look at the TV!" I exclaimed.

The voice-over announced, "Saturday night is a special night! Staci Whitaker, Caleb Taveras, Jack Deluca, and featuring Celeste Hernandez in the television premiere, beginning at 8 Eastern, 7 Central...only on The Gold Entertainment Channel."

Everyone laughed.

"Hey, I need to record that one! By the way, who are those folks anyway?" I joked.

"You silly!" teased Staci.

"Like old times!" I responded. "I need to record that one!"

After setting the DVR to record Staci and Celeste's upcoming movie, I continued flipping through the channels. Then, my cell phone blared a notification sound.

"Wow! That was loud!" commented Staci.

"Looks like Jamie sent me a text."

"Wonder what it is?"

I read, "News alert! InterCable News! Watch now! Live coverage from LA!"

"Uh-oh. I wonder what's happening back home."

I switched over to InterCable News. From what we could see, they had the news alert and news feed scrolling banners. We had caught the middle of a breaking news report.

The news anchor said, "Over the Century City neighborhood of Los Angeles. Hazmat teams arrived with paramedics and police to quarantine this office building. At approximately 10:10 a.m. Pacific Daylight Time, a 911 call was made from the PRI International's office on the 5th floor of the Constitution Insurance Building in Century City. Again, this is in the Century City neighborhood of Los Angeles. The area has a mixed use of office buildings, retail stores, and residential apartments and condominiums. It's on the Westside from downtown Los Angeles in Southern California. As you can see on the graphic where this is occurring, live, west of downtown LA. The Century Towers complex is nearby."

"PRI International is a well-known public relations and promotional services firm with many offices throughout the United States and the world. One of their services is handling fan mail for a variety of Hollywood celebrities. The exact number of clients is unknown at this time. What we do know is that at approximately 10:05 a.m. Pacific Daylight Time, a PRI employee opened an envelope from a sorted stack of fan mail. In the process, an unknown fine white powder spilled from the envelope. Upon the discovery, another PRI employee called 911 to report the powder to police. Building security was notified by LAPD to evacuate all offices in the building. Unfortunately, members of the immediately affected office area of PRI on the 5th floor...those office suites were told to remain quarantined until Hazmat and paramedics could make their way to their office area. Employees from the building's other tenants were told to evacuate immediately and not return to the building until further notice. Those persons were also told to 'not take anything with them out of the building. Leave all items behind.' Concerns have been raised if any of the white powder could've become airborne and spread from the PRI...uh...PRI 5th floor offices... PRI hasn't revealed to whom the affected letter was addressed. We hope to learn the identity of the intended receiver... We're now going to listen in on KLAT-TV's local coverage to see what they are telling their viewers...'"

Another news anchor began, "Has received the following statement from...uh...PRI has released a statement that says 'our employees followed established protocol when an unexpected and unidentified powder was found in a piece of fan mail earlier today approximately 10:05 a.m. Our prayers and thoughts are with the affected employees.'"

"Now reports from our sources don't have the names of the affected employees. We've been told that they've been taken to an undisclosed LA hospital for quarantine and testing. Hazmat authorities are checking air quality throughout the building to determine if any harmful particles could be detected. It's reported that Hazmat specialists are in... the particular PRI office on the 5th floor where the envelope spilled the unidentified powdery substance. Testing...testing is underway to determine its nature..."

The InterCable news anchor returned. "This is InterCable News with a breaking news alert repeating once again in Century City in Los Angeles bringing you live coverage from our local affiliate KLAT..."

"PRI?" asked Staci. "Is that the firm Celeste contracted for her PR and fan mail?"

"Yeah. I wonder what else Jamie knows." I texted him. *What relevance does this news story have to us?*

As we continued to watch the overhead circling of the office building and the continuous breaking news story from the news anchor, Jamie texted back a few minutes later.

"Oh no! Jamie says the affected letter was addressed to Celeste Hernandez." I flinched.

"Oh my! He must know more about the situation."

Celeste walked into the room. "What's going on?"

"PRI International is the PR firm that you're using, right?" I asked Celeste.

"Yes, what happened?" answered Celeste.

"Breaking news story," I said, "somebody pulled what appears to be a dangerous prank at their LA office."

I whispered to Staci and Celeste, "Celeste's mail was targeted. I'd keep that hush until we know more."

As I kept the TV on the breaking news coverage, I wondered what would happen next. After about thirty minutes, we decided to turn back to The Gold Entertainment Channel and the show that was on. The promo for Staci' and Celeste's movie appeared again during one of the commercial breaks. I had to smile because Celeste really looked nice in her new TV movie role.

Celeste had left the living room at some point during the TV movie. It seemed like hours had gone by, but I looked and only two hours had passed. As I was about to get up from my recliner, my phone buzzed a warning text message from Jamie Caballero. This was no ordinary text message. Jamie's message was to alert us that we had a potentially dangerous situation and to call him immediately. I reached for my phone and called. Staci jumped when the alert sounded. She looked at me after she looked at her phone.

"Is Jamie alerting all of us?" asked Staci.

"I'm calling him," I said. "Something major must've developed in the last couple of hours."

"Hello, Mike," Jamie quickly answered.

"What's up?"

"Glad you were near your phone. We have more trouble."

"Ok, let me put you on the speaker. Staci is with me."

Jamie asked, "Where are you at the moment?"

"In my living room, in Plano. Celeste is in the other room. Staci and Kyle are also here. All of the kids are here visiting."

"I just received word from Staci's hired PR firm in Studio City, about three fan letters in the last couple of days," said Jamie. "Her firm was alerted because two of the envelopes were missing return addresses. Another envelope had a similar M.O. The third letter had a return address that has been determined to be bogus. All three letters made references to knowing Staci has been visiting in the Dallas area the last few days. One of the letters specifically stated Plano. One of the envelopes had a suspicious stain on it. Unfortunately, there were death threats in the letters."

"Oh, Dear Precious Lord, that's all we need now!" I agonized.

"Jamie, Kyle, and I need to return to LA in a couple of days," admitted Staci.

Jamie advised, "You need to stay put until the authorities can do more investigating. The one letter with a bogus return address in Plano, Texas. The postmark on that letter was Dallas."

"What about the stained envelope?" asked Staci.

"Postal inspectors, the FBI, and the LAPD are all on it. Texas authorities have also been called to be on the lookout. There was no powder found in the envelope like what happened earlier today in Century City. Do you want me to get some officers over there for protection?"

"I don't want a media circus here in Texas," I objected. "I watched the footage for nearly thirty minutes after your text."

"We can't take any chances," fretted Jamie. "If someone is attempting to harm any of you, we need to stop them before—"

"I get it!" I exclaimed. "If they're here in the DFW area, I don't want more media attention here."

"Mike, I was just thinking…" began Jamie.

"I understand your concern. Many people know Staci and I are from here. Someone pulling a prank like this is scary. I'm not going to let them scare me."

Jamie cautioned, "Okay. Look, if you have any trouble there, be prepared to make the call."

"Jamie, we'll stay close by. I'll alert our local bodyguards."

"I've already alerted them," confirmed Jamie. "If you need to leave the house, we'll make sure that they're available before any of you travel outside your gated community."

"I don't like the feeling of being in a cage!" I admitted.

"This is only temporary. The hype usually subsides if investigators discover the responsible parties…I hope," commented Jamie.

"Keep in touch."

"Mom's calling," Staci said, looking at her phone. As she answered, she walked into the next room to take the call.

"Your parents and all immediate family members have been contacted as a precaution through the special emergency app," said Jamie.

"I can only assume they're at home. They were earlier today."

"It looks like your mom's calling Staci. I'll let all of you discuss further what you want to do. If you plan to go out in public, please make sure the bodyguards are with you. We don't need more trouble."

"Thanks, Jamie," "I said.

"One other item. Another church canceled you and Celeste."

"I know. That is the twelfth church this month!"

"This fallout has been wild."

"Keep us posted. We'll talk later."

I walked over to Staci to share Jamie's message. Celeste and Staci couldn't believe the devastation this whole escapade had caused. Jamie had texted what one church had sent him.

"You aren't going to show that to Celeste, are you?" asked Staci.

"If I didn't, I would be lying to her."

Staci handed me back my cell phone. I made my way to the kitchen. Celeste was watching Elizabeth, Carmen, and Amy playing a board game. Kyle was outside with Joe and Alex.

"I guess everyone received the alert," I declared.

"Kyle left his phone on the counter," disclosed Celeste. "He's outside with the boys."

I whispered, "I need to tell you quickly what's going on. I don't want to bother the kids." Celeste followed me out of the kitchen.

"PRI isn't the only one affected. Postal inspectors and FBI are also involved. No suspects. Three more envelopes—one with a mysterious unknown stain— were delivered to Staci's PR office in Studio City. Suspicious letters. Two lacked return addresses. The third one had a bogus return address. All three envelopes contained letters claiming that the sender knew Staci was visiting the Dallas area. One of the three stated specifically she was visiting Plano. All three of these letters contained death threats. Hence, we'll need to call the security team if any of us go in public, until the danger has subsided."

"All over this?"

"I know. I've had enough of this."

I walked away from Celeste. She could tell that I was very peeved by all these developments. I quickly made my way to a hidden room in our house.

As I removed a hidden panel, I accessed my gun safe. My cousin Dan had owned this gun safe for years. He and his wife were moving into a condo sometime back. He didn't want the guns and gun safe to be sold. He knew I was an avid hunter in the four-state area of Arkansas, Louisiana, Oklahoma, and Texas. As I closed the safe door, Celeste entered. She was very surprised when she saw me with a gun in my hand.

"Michael!" scolded Celeste. "Where'd you get that gun?"

"Birthday number eighteen," I chuckled. "What a beaut!"

"More guns? And a hidden gun safe?" asked Celeste. "Where'd you get all of this?"

"My folks kept a home here in north Texas, and we kept this gun out of California," I quipped.

"You aren't going to pack 'heat' around here?" asked Celeste. "Are you?"

"Celeste, we have some unnamed folks going around threatening you and Staci…" I began.

"This is outrageous…," said Celeste.

"No, it's just me putting on the 'Full Armor of God.' I chuckled, "I don't have a sword. This is the next best thing!"

"I don't feel comfortable with…" trailed Celeste.

"Celeste, I've been handling guns for a long time. My cousin Dan and I went deer hunting in my teens up in Oklahoma and Arkansas. Besides, where da ya think all of that 'burger' meat came from this past winter?" I asked. "Did you forget that I didn't buy that mount in the living room from a rummage sale or swipe it from a prop room?"

Celeste looked stunned. I admitted to her, "You know I've had it since I was sixteen. Came from a hunting trip in southwest Arkansas."

"We aren't talking about hunting deer!"

"No, but I know what I'm doing, when it comes to a gun. Let's face it. You can take the boy out of Texas, but you can't take Texas out of the boy!"

"Why won't you simply let the police do their job?"

"The police will do their job. I'll let 'em do it. I'm a Texan! This is Texas! I'd prefer to have my opportunity to stop someone before anything gets out of hand."

Celeste continued looking concerned.

"I don't have any swords." I pointed to my gun. "This is the modern version of my 'Sword of the Spirit' *[Ephesians 6:17]*."

"Michael!" scolded Celeste. "Paul also says that "'Vengeance is God's decision, not yours.' *[Romans 12:19]*."

"You're right. Whoever these folks are won't get a chance to take any of us out. Although God is there, I'm not God. I can't see all, know all, and read men's hearts. I have to be prepared."

"Oh, Mike!"

"I have my shoulder holster so I can hide it under my sport coats, and my concealed carry permit is valid. I think these bulletproof vests will fit, and I may have enough."

"Bulletproof vests?"

"Modern day version and literal presentation of the 'Breastplate of Righteousness!' *[Ephesians 6:14]*."

"You're being ridiculous and getting carried away with this!"

"The vest does attempt to protect the heart! In a much different way! If I don't have enough, the bodyguards might know where to get more quickly."

"By the way, Jamie sent me a text. A twelfth church meeting has been canceled."

"A twelfth one?!"

"You don't want to know what that church said."

"They said something in addition to simply canceling?"

I retrieved my cell phone, pulled up Jamie's text message, and gave Celeste my phone. "Tell Mike and his...Jezebel...we're canceling until she and his sister repent! Revelation 2:20." Celeste lowered her head. "Oh no!"

"Yep. Jamie tried to explain to them the situation. They aren't going to budge until they hear or receive a confession directly from us. They want one from Staci as well."

"What about that video of you?"

"It's been running rampant all over the Internet the last couple of weeks."

We recognized the reference to Revelation 2:20. From the NASB version, it reads, *"But I have this against you, that you tolerate the woman Jezebel, who calls herself a prophetess, and she teaches and leads My bond-servants astray so that they commit acts of immorality and eat things sacrificed to idols."*

"What are we going to do?" asked Celeste.

"We're gonna have to fight back."

Our home office phone rang shortly thereafter. Celeste went to answer it, and I quickly closed up the hidden room.

"Hello?" said Celeste. "Yes. We'll accept the call. Let me put him on the speakerphone." Celeste switched on the speakerphone as I closed the office door. "Karl, Mike and I are so glad to hear from you."

Karl Ramirez had been a practicing Southern California attorney for more than twenty years. He joined his father and older brother in their West Hollywood law firm. Many stars had been their clients for many years. Karl's dad, Enrique, had built quite a reputation in nearly forty years in Southern Cal. I remembered Mom, Dad,

Staci, and I would meet with Enrique to discuss contracts and modify various provisions.

As Karl spoke with us, he believed that we had two legitimate cases. He suggested that he file on behalf of Celeste an emotional duress lawsuit against FibreTainment, the studio, and other members of the production staff, including executive producer Albert Jacobs. Karl also suggested we file a separate lawsuit for compensation and punitive damages for our motivational speaking company. Celeste and I booked a few motivation speaking events individually and jointly throughout the year at various churches around Texas and the country. Since *"Goodwin Circles Around Again"* debuted, twelve churches had canceled so far. The separate lawsuit against FibreTainment, the studio, the production company, and Albert Jacobs, would address our independent-but-related business unfairly losing revenue from the fallout.

I asked Karl if there was a way to prevent the studio from firing Staci or Celeste if they wanted to issue a confession, or apologize for the way the whole situation had unfolded. I told him that we needed that immediately. At the current rate, Celeste and I were going to eventually lose more opportunities—possibly permanently. If we lost too many, we would most likely have to close our motivational speaking business. Karl said that he'd get to work on the injunction. In the meantime, I wanted to talk with our church to see how we could get our message out on a possible confession. Over the next few days, our family planned what we would say if we had to speak at church.

10

THE GOOD NEWS BECOMES
THE BIG NEWS

◆ ———— ◆ ———— ◆

By Wednesday, Karl Ramirez had drafted an emergency injunction order to prevent FibreTainment, the studio, and certain key people of the production team—including executive producer Albert Jacobs—from firing Staci and Celeste because we wished to issue a confession on our own. This would give us time to prepare our talk.

On the local front, I called Justin Lockwood to discuss plans of us coming forward on Sunday morning. We devised that we would work in conjunction with our sister congregation of Spring Creek Community Bible Church in Southern California—Staci and Kyle's church. With the two-hour differential, coordinating the shared broadcast would require some ingenuity. The plan would be to coordinate our 11:00 a.m. Sunday morning service in Texas to coincide with our sister church's 9:00 a.m. service in California via video Web streaming. Our church would watch and participate with our California brethren's worship team over the Web as one body in Christ. Both churches would switch to Texas to carry Justin Lockwood's special message on Romans 14 and 15. Both churches websites would simulcast the live stream. There would be no announcement that Staci, Celeste, and I would be present. We didn't want to cause a media frenzy at the church. We would enter the sanctuary through a back-door entrance during the service. Our family would worship in a side room near the sanctuary, and the three of us would come out on Justin's cue, following his sermon, to share our message.

Only one Dallas area TV station would be called to record the event as a backup and to cover the story. For those ten years on the network, our show was carried on the American SuperChannel Network. Although we hadn't had a show on that network in nearly twelve years, building a sense of nostalgia for our fans was the idea for our local friends and church family who remembered tuning in locally each Friday night to KSFD. I remember doing those many local promos encouraging all to "Tune in to our hometown SuperChannel affiliate, KSFD, Fort Worth-Dallas." It may have given my six-year-old self the inspiration to go into voice-over acting.

On Friday, we received word that an emergency injunction was in place. Jamie had pulled a few strings to speed up the process with the LA court. The showrunners and show owners couldn't fire Staci and Celeste under their current contracts with the injunction in place. Celeste was very determined to end her contract after season two became available. I prayed for everyone's protection during the next few weeks and months.

Finally, Sunday morning rolled around. Staci, Kyle, their kids, and our parents drove over to our house early that morning. We had a good breakfast to prepare for the testimonies that Celeste, Staci, and I would give before the congregations and the world. No one at the church—other than the upper teaching team pastors and Justin Lockwood—would know we'd be there. Our elders were put on alert to make sure that no one in the audience who might look suspicious could attempt to do anything. While

Celeste wasn't crazy about the idea, I had my Texas version of the "Sword of the Spirit" tucked under my sport coat in its holster and ready to use at a moment's notice.

Around 10:30 a.m., my family and I jumped into our SUV. Kyle, Staci, their kids, and our parents jumped into their rental SUV and followed us to the church. Kyle's mom and Celeste's parents were unable to attend the church service in Plano. They'd sent best wishes to us and prayed for a safe and successful service and testimonies. While we were in commute, I decided to turn on the radio to see what was happening in the news.

The network news came on around 10:35 a.m. The typical news stories were abuzz on the national scene. After the commercial break, the news returned to share some entertainment news. What we heard next, we were in for a shock.

The radio news announcer began, "In the entertainment business, SYZ Studios released early this morning that executive producer and creator of the TV series '*Goodwin Circle*,' Albert Jacobs, has been fired. More from Hollywood."

Another news reporter began, "Many Gen Xer's remember the antics of Robin and Davey Goodwin on the popular TV sitcom '*Goodwin Circle*.' Created by TV producer Albert Jacobs as a wholesome family sitcom, that sitcom had a near-decade run. Jacobs was showrunner of the recent FibreTainment distributed series '*Goodwin Circles Around Again*,' a modern sequel of his previous 1988 series. SYZ and FibreTainment both refused to comment on any particular details of why the sixty-nine-year-old former actor-turned-writer, executive, and show creator was let go. However, sources under conditions of anonymity claim that Jacobs has been accused of multiple sexual harassment incidents among some show staffers before and during the current show's production. Sources claim that, to their knowledge, none of the show's principal actors—Staci Whitman-Carella and Celeste Hernandez, and the young actresses playing their on-screen daughters—were among the accusers. Requests for comment from the actresses' representatives were unanswered at this time. Speculation is brewing that an injunction filed in Los Angeles County Superior Court on Friday by legal representatives for the two actresses might be related. Other sources hinted that three lawsuits are expected to be heard in the next few days or weeks. Filings with the LA Superior Court list LA-based entertainment attorney Karl Ramirez's name on the lawsuits. Staci Whitaker-Carella and Celeste Hernandez are listed on separate files. Celeste Hernandez and her husband—former TV child actor Michael Whitman—are listed jointly on a third file. The exact details have not been provided at this time."

The first news announcer said, "Listeners may remember in the 1980s, the real-life Whitman sister-brother duo portrayed the main sister-brother duo—Robin and Davey Goodwin—on the SYZ Studios series 'Goodwin Circle,' that aired a ten-year run as part of the ASC Network's Friday night comedy block. Michael Whitman would meet his eventual off-screen wife Celeste Hernandez on the series. On the show, Michael's character, Davey Goodwin, fell in love with Robin's friend Debbie near the last few seasons of the show. The original "Goodwin Circle" continues to air in syndication and Web streamed by various services around the world."

The second news announcer said, "The updated series 'Goodwin Circles Around Again' made its debut earlier this year to very mixed-to-negative reviews. Various Christian groups have expressed outrage over the new show's unexpected raunchy and coarse content. Both actresses Staci Whitman-Carella and Celeste Hernandez have expressed their views as conservative Christians. Past detractors have expressed dislike for the fundamentalist views of the three actors. Earlier this spring, a video went viral circulating on the Internet of an angry and profanity-laden Michael Whitman rant expressing outrage over an abortion issue. The video was taken by a third party after one of Whitman's motivation seminars nine years ago. Last week, Michael Whitman's representatives issued an apology."

Around 10:50 a.m., we arrived at Spring Creek Community Bible Church. We drove to a back entrance. I stopped and parked the car. Kyle and family followed behind us and did the same. I shut off the car and sprang to the back door to knock on it. A church usher opened the door and recognized me. I motioned everyone to exit the vehicles and make their way to the door.

Once inside, Kyle, Mom, and Dad spent their time watching the kids. Staci, Celeste, and I reviewed our notes once more. Special seating had been set up in the side room. This is where we would sit during the service until called to present our testimonies. Justin Lockwood came to see us before the service. We could hear people in the sanctuary.

"Are you guys ready?" asked Justin.

I joked, "I'd say, 'y'all ready?'"

"Nice reminder that we're in Texas." smiled Justin. "We're about ten minutes away from the service's start."

To help us know what was going on during the service, the technical crew had set up a TV monitor that would show the same feed as the sanctuary's two large screens.

"I feel a little nervous," said Staci.

"Not the time to get stage fright," I quipped. "Christ is with us on this."

"I'm glad that we took the time to write down what we planned to say. I really messed up at that last college testimony."

"It's interesting that whole room of college students, a few theology professors, and many other guests missed it.

Only one minister approached you after the service to explain what you did."

"You're the only one that watched online that caught it as well."

"It'll be interesting to see what reaction that anecdote will receive."

The time had arrived. We all made our way to our seats. The worship service began as the worship leader welcomed everyone. The music was wonderful, and we sang three hymns. A few announcements were made. A prayer and offering and music came next.

Finally, the screen faded. Then, a special animation appeared to remind everyone of today's message. When I saw it, I thought it looked vaguely familiar. Then, it hit me. The Special Sermon Presentation screen animation was reminiscent of the animation title card that the ASC Network used back in the 1980s to announce TV specials, when a regularly scheduled TV program wouldn't be seen that night but would return the following week at its usual time.

After the animation stopped, a voice announced, "The originally scheduled 9:00 a.m. Sunday Sermon will not be seen and heard today. In its place, a special sermon presentation from our fellow church in Plano, Texas. Our 9:00 a.m. service's sermon will return at its usual time next week, live during our weekly service...at 12:00 p.m. Eastern, 11:00 a.m. Central, and 9:00 a.m. Pacific...on this live stream."

I heard a few laughs from the audience. I looked among my family. Some of them thought the animation was cute and brought a lot of smiles. We remembered many times that we saw that special presentation screen. Staci and I participated in a few specials on the network as ourselves. It was very funny to see this send up.

The animation screen faded away to show Justin Lockwood. He welcomed everyone again. He explained what was going on with the reference to a 9:00 a.m. service. He also did a special shout-out to our church friends in California and everyone else on the Web joining us. He shared how he thought this was a neat time for us to join together today for this service. The special message today had a significance to not only our churches but also to our church families. Before entering the sermon, he asked that we all bow our heads in prayer. After a brief pause, Justin prayed, then he asked all to turn in their Bibles to Romans 14 and Romans 15:1. Justin then spent about fifteen to twenty minutes on a sermon about what Romans 14 through Romans 15:1 means. He hinted to the recent news items; people arguing over picture posts on social media by famous people without mentioning any particular names. As he neared the end of his expository teaching, he began the transition from the Scripture to the real example.

"How many of you remember the TV show *'Goodwin Circle'* back in the '80s?" Justin asked, "Okay. I see many hands. Many of you know it's still seen on TV in reruns. Back in the day, we had to wait a whole week for another episode. Rerunning TV shows has become a big business. Speaking of *'Goodwin Circle'* do you remember the main kids? Look at this picture. I believe this is from 1995. Take a look at this. Recognize anyone?"

The screen changed to show a picture of Terrence Forrester, Marian Deavers, Staci, Celeste, and me. It was shot on the living room set on our old soundstage at SYZ Studios. The hairstyles and clothing had that late-'80s-early '90s look. We looked so young in that picture.

"As you can see, the main characters from that time. Many of you may remember Staci and Mike Whitman. They're no longer kids. In fact, they're married...oops, I mean...married to their own spouses." There was some laughter from the audience.

Justin continued, "And they have kids of their own. Of course, Mike Whitman and Celeste Hernandez got married in real life." The screen changed to a wedding picture of Celeste and me.

Justin asked, "Did you know that Staci and Mike are native Texans?" Some of the audience seem to acknowledge knowing. "They grew up in their very early lives here in Plano. I have read an audition was held in Dallas in 1986 for that TV show began their journey. Now, Staci lives in California once again. Mike and Celeste moved back here to Texas many years ago. Staci and Kyle, her husband, are involved with our church in California; Mike and Celeste were at one time, as well as Staci and Mike's parents."

"Several years ago, Mike wanted to return to Texas when Hollywood projects didn't meet his needs or desires. He and his family moved back. Today, Mike is a local voice-over artist and a traveling Christian motivational speaker; visiting churches and other conferences, and sharing his testimony for Christ. Today, we've a special message he has to share. Ladies and Gentlemen, please give a welcome to our hometown friend…Mike Whitman!"

The audience clapped. I stood up from my seat and looked at Celeste. She looked at me with a wink of approval. I looked to Staci who then looked at me. She gave me a big smile. I walked out of the room. Suddenly, I was on the stage with Justin Lockwood and shaking his hand. I noticed on a monitor that they showed a camera shot of the California congregation, who was watching. I also heard a few cheers. As I approached the pulpit, the applause and cheers subsided. The church's broadcast team superimposed my name on sanctuary projection screens during the beginning of my talk.

"Well, good morning, Spring Creek-Texas. Good morning, Spring Creek-SoCal. Well, this is a special day. I'm glad to see all of you. As Justin said, Plano is my hometown; although I called California home for a few years."

I continued, "It seems like only yesterday on a May afternoon in 1993, that Staci and I both decided that we would accept Jesus Christ as our Lord and Savior. Our lives have never been the same since. Many of you know or have heard some of my testimony before about how that happened. What you may not know is life since the *'Goodwin Circle'* show hasn't been easy. Voice-over acting is more what I do now for various commercials and industrial videos. However, I have fun doing that. As Justin said, I have a special message to share. By the way, it's free."

Some in the audience laughed. "I'm here to declare, before God and all, that I've committed two sins. I'm not happy about it. First, a viral video has been making its runs through the Internet the last few weeks. I ask that you forgive me what that video shows. I became very irate nine years ago with a conference participant who wouldn't stop demanding that I accept the pro-choice abortion stance. The video shows me in a negative way because I became very loud and angry. I let a few profanity-laced words escape my mouth when the discussion after a presentation became heated. I ask for your forgiveness." I could hear some in the audience give their approval.

"Also, I failed as a husband," I began. I heard gasps. "It's not that." A few laughed. "Instead, I failed to allow my wife to share any concerns about the new TV show that recently debuted. That show called *'Goodwin Circles Around Again'*...and bites you in the rear." The audience laughed.

"By that reaction, I suspect some of you know where this is going and how I feel about this new show. I didn't allow Celeste to tell me any plotlines of the show. She stayed true. When we sat down at the TV a few weeks ago, I couldn't watch past the first fifteen minutes of the first episode. Too much ungodly content hit me. I turned to Celeste who had said a prayer before we watched. She called for my protection. I saw why. Celeste sat there with her eyes closed for much of the time as I watched that show. She acted like she was dying inside by having to relive those scenes all of those weeks later."

"I must also admit that I pushed her to watch the show that night. I'd been warned by a friend earlier in the day trouble brewing around the show. Here I was, watching it nearly a month after the premiere. I hadn't been reading any of the trade papers to see any news about the show. No one told me anything about it until then. I'd been too busy at work to think anything about it."

"In closing, I ask for forgiveness for not allowing my wife the freedom to tell me what was troubling her during those weeks of taping in California. I'll never require her to keep a plotline away from me if trouble should arise again. However, Celeste will tell you. We'll never allow her to be unprotected, without some restrictions about what she will and won't do on a television show. We won't allow another bait-and-switch to happen like this again. Thank you."

The congregations clapped and cheered. As I walked to the chair on stage left, stage crews were bringing another chair next to me where Celeste would sit. The congregations quieted as Justin Lockwood returned to the portable pulpit.

"That shows you that many things can happen behind the scenes in the lives of actors in a television show," Justin observed. "For you, Mike, we're praying for you and your family. Speaking of family, Mike mentioned his wife, Celeste. Our next testimony is from that very person, Celeste Hernandez."

The congregations clapped and cheered again. This time, Celeste appeared on stage and made her way to the pulpit. As the applause and cheers subsided, Celeste gently grasped Justin's hand as a greeting. Justin stepped away to allow Celeste to the pulpit. The church's broadcast team superimposed Celeste's name on the screens during the beginning of her talk.

"Good morning to everyone in Texas and in California. I appreciate you providing us the opportunity to share with you these concerns. As Justin told you, I've been married to Mike Whitman for sixteen years. We met in 1995 on the set of *'Goodwin Circle.'* Over the next few years, we became closer friends. Mike wanted to keep me on the show because he saw something in me. When I learned that Mike was a Christian, I could see that he wanted someone who understood that faith. In 1998 when the show ended, Mike and I were dating. We continued to see each other in some small acting projects for a while until Mike proposed in 1999. We married in 2000. We have three wonderful children—two girls and one boy—and they're a blessing to us."

"Of course, children are a main concern for us. Mike and I have tried to provide and exemplify a godly and Christian home for them. With Mike's and God's help over these last several years, we've led and taught our kids to know and love the Lord. While we've focused on that, I had no idea that a new TV show would cause trouble, and I'd become part of that trouble. When we began shooting the show in 2015, we didn't know that the show would take the dark and gritty turn. We had a first pilot with Terrence Forrester and Marian Deavers playing my TV in-laws. Mike was unable at the time to come to California to participate in the tapings and reprise his role of son Davey Goodwin. The plan was to have his character be on a business trip or elsewhere. He was just somewhere else, other than at home. After the first pilot, the show was quickly tested. We were told that we had to do a reshoot because the test audience didn't like it. A new set of writers were hired. We also had some unexpected cast changes. Staci and I were locked into our contracts. The second pilot tested better with the test audiences. Unfortunately, this version of the show was much darker and coarser. It had some strong language with words that I didn't like using. Staci and I tried to negotiate some of the content out of the show. We were unable to rid a lot of it. After taping two seasons of this wilder and more adult format, I was completely ready to come home. After the show debuted, I wasn't sure what Mike would think. When he finally viewed the first episode, I knew there was going to be trouble. I finally burst into tears with Mike. I knew that the show was a failure. I had to promote the show as stipulated in my contract. I'll announce today that if the show doesn't change its content, I won't return for season three...," said Celeste.

The congregations cheered.

"My reason for sharing all of this is to provide a confession to all of you. I shouldn't have allowed myself to compromise our Christian values that Mike and I've held dear for so long. I let people encourage me to compromise. Therefore, I ask you and God today to forgive me for the mistakes that I made. I confess that I was wrong to continue participating with this show. I apologize for misleading anyone into watching, expecting a family show. I won't let this situation happen again. I'll also make sure that I have all production and plot points in writing and agreed before starring in another project. Thank you."

Celeste walked from the pulpit to the empty chair beside me as the congregations applauded. Justin returned to the pulpit.

"Again, Celeste shows that sometimes we don't know all of the facts. Now, we know that a contract was involved where she couldn't make an apology or anything that could jeopardize the show. Finally, we have Mike's sister and Celeste's sister-in-law. You may remember her as the oldest Goodwin child from 'Goodwin Circle'—Robin Goodwin. All the way from Southern California, Spring

Creek-Texas, and Spring Creek-SoCal, please welcome Staci Whitaker-Carella."

This time, Staci appeared onstage and made her way to the pulpit. As the applause and cheers subsided, she grasped Justin's hand as a greeting and then stepped behind the pulpit. She took a deep breath because she was a little nervous.

"Good morning...Texas...and...California...I'm not reading from a script..." Laughs could be heard from the audience. "Or a teleprompter...or cue cards...I only have a few prepared notes with me so I can stay on track..." Staci looked to Justin with a mock puzzled look. "Who cued the laugh track?"

I could tell that Staci was nervous about what she was going to say. "I'm not here to tell jokes. When I was asked—when all three of us were asked to come back and do this new show, I wasn't sure if it would work. Mike was too busy to do it when we started. When he encouraged Celeste to do it if she wanted, we were under the impression that Mike might make a few guest visits. We had an initial pilot show—a first test episode, that would've followed an updated format with our characters. My husband was also unable to reprise his role. We pretended that both Davey Goodwin and Bryan Brandenburg, who was played by my real-life husband, Kyle, in the two TV movies were off at work or on business trips. There was some uncertainty if Kyle would be able to return as my on-screen husband. We had some talk of recasting. When the test audience didn't respond well to that first pilot, changes were made rather quickly. Somehow, without our knowledge, the show's tone and direction changed. Since we were contractually obligated, Celeste and I had to do the show."

"I've had fans suggest that Kyle should discipline me. One person posted on my social media account, when I commented about my relationship with Kyle, suggested he should give me a good spanking." The audience laughed at that idea when Staci gave a bewildered look.

"I can't get a break. Whatever I post or say, no one's happy. That's ridiculous! We thought we knew our crew. Every time that we saw the new scripts, Celeste and I were wondering when this show was going to end and why we were still wanting to do this. After the reported death in Tennessee, we realized we needed to make a decision. During the taping of those two seasons back-to-back, I thought the storylines would get better. I thought I could negotiate in removing more of the content or toning some of it down. At the end of the day and after seeing all of the arguments that have been said from fellow Christians, having many people scream at my immediate and extended family, and extended family members also sharing their disapproval of the show's content, I've come to the conclusion that I made a big mistake. I should've put my foot down like I did those many years ago for my brother Mike. Back then, the writers and executive producer tried to put Mike's character in a very demoralizing situation in one episode. Back then, a fellow believer Gerald Knobele, who was a network executive at the time, had our back. If Gerald Knobele hadn't been there, our careers might have turned out differently. He sided with us when we felt the storyline was inappropriate."

"Unfortunately, we didn't have a 'Gerald Knobele' to help Celeste and me to stop some of the crazy story ideas on this new show. I was forced to parrot all of that crazy language and pretended to do some really stupid things. I've learned my lesson. I'll have to be much more restrictive in my future contracts if I am going to work for certain companies again. I ask that you please forgive me for the actions, behavior, and attitude that you saw me acting in those shows. Please also forgive me for the pride and arrogance that I've shown in some of my interviews about the show. As part of my contract, I was required to promote *'Goodwin Circles Around Again.'* I couldn't let on any troubled feelings that I really had. I've had to ask forgiveness from my family for some of the attitude and behaviors that apparently were influencing my own behavior. In other words, some of Robin's bad traits were rubbing off into my real life. When I sent a text message to all of my real family members about Mike's inappropriate video, it took Mike, Celeste, Mom, and Dad to let me know how inappropriate that was. I had inadvertently reenacted a plotline from one of the recent TV episodes. When I wouldn't listen to my family, my husband Kyle and I had to have a serious talk. He had to set some things straight. He lovingly brought God's Word to me. Through Kyle, God spoke to me where I was wrong."

"I also ask for forgiveness for a doctrine error that I made at a recent college meeting. I made a statement encouraging fellow believers that they need to be able to work outside a Christian environment. There are times that you won't always be insulated by a Christian bubble. You can't be naïve about the world. Unfortunately, I implied to some that if we, the Christian believers, aren't in all of those places...in the world...even the dark places...that unbelievers would take those jobs and roles. Therefore, we as believers need to be there regardless... Apparently, I implied...that believers should take a job...even if it compromises our personal Christian principles and beliefs."

"Following the meeting, a local pastor who works with the college shared with me that I had made a mistake. In my haste, I didn't consider this error since I was so focused in trying to convince the students that I was still a Christian. Pastor Jeff, that's what I'll call him here...because I didn't ask permission to give his full name, shared this truth. In a *perfect* world, it would be biblical to encourage all to go out into the world and take jobs with no restrictions. However, Pastor Jeff reminded me that we unfortunately live...in a *fallen* world...where sin runs rampant and the devil currently has a growing influence."

"Since Satan has been gaining this influence, I've tried to be on my guard. If I'm told to do anything contrary to the Gospel that I've been taught and have read, I shouldn't participate or encourage the devil's work [1 Peter 5:8-9]. I've been reading the Bible and trying to focus as much as possible on God's Word while outside of the acting jobs. I didn't want to lose focus. Unfortunately, I made the mistake…that I shouldn't encourage my fellow believers to do as I did. I blindly accepted an acting job with a crew that I thought I knew [Psalms 118:8, Jeremiah 17:5, Proverbs 3:5-6, 2 Timothy 3:13-17, Psalms 146:3]. As a result, I got stuck. I should've known better then. I should've known better when I told the college students to go out into this world and accept opportunities without considering where they were. Were those in charge truly for God or for Satan? Psalms 118:5-9 seems to fit my current situation."

Suddenly, Staci stopped talking. She looked straight ahead. Celeste and I were bewildered. I heard people in the audience murmuring. Many were uncertain what was going to happen next. I heard a few members whisper, "Is she alright?" "What's going on?"

"Oh!" moaned Staci. "Dear, Precious Lord!"

Staci closed her eyes and lowered her head. She began crying. Kyle walked onstage. As he approached her, he wrapped his arms around Staci.

Staci turned back to the congregation with open tear-filled eyes. "It's okay. I'm fine… Ladies and Gentlemen…this is my husband, Kyle, for those that may not remember or know. Thank you, Kyle."

Kyle stayed with Staci with his arm around her back, and she continued, "As I was saying, I've made some mistakes. I don't know why I didn't see it before. As we all know, Jesus was betrayed within mere hours of leaving the Upper Room with the Disciples. Judas Iscariot received thirty pieces of silver *[Matthew 26:14-16]*...and not too long ago...and miles from here...I accepted more than thirty pieces of silver...and ended up...betraying my Lord... although I was playing a character...I accepted an acting role...on a TV show...whose content and actions caused me...to betray my Lord..."

Staci teared up and with a crack in her voice said, "Lord, I ask and seek your forgiveness...for my selfishness, pride, arrogance, and... greed. To my fellow believers, I humbly ask for your forgiveness...for what I've put many of you through."

Staci turned and hugged Kyle. From what I could see, the first few rows of people appeared to be a mix of mesmerized, shocked, and stunned. Many were shedding tears. Many were realizing that this fellow believer had been tricked and forced into a difficult situation. There was a sudden calm among those in the congregation in Texas. We could slightly hear some of the audio from California. I thought I heard a few cheers, a few voices say, "Go, Staci!" and some voices shouted, "Thank you, Jesus!"

After what seemed like an eternity, Staci turned back to the audience while still embracing Kyle, and said, "Thank you."

There was a brief silence. We could see again one of the large monitors and hear the California congregation over the speakers begin to clap and cheer. Both congregations joined in. Celeste and I made our way toward Staci. Our family gathered there at our church in Plano on that Sunday afternoon.

Justin walked back to the pulpit. "Thank you, Staci. Ladies and Gentlemen. Brothers and Sisters in Christ. I can't recall of a time in ministry when I've seen three believers of the same family come forward to make a public confession. These families have been through a whole lot the last two years. They've had to endure public scrutiny, ridicule, and questions about their faith. I know that Staci and Celeste have had to endure the unfortunate personal battle of being placed in a difficult situation. I ask that our church here in Texas, there in California, and to all throughout the world who are watching through the Webcast, I ask that you please pray for these families. While they have felt the need to publicly confess what they've had to struggle and endure, the battle isn't over yet. If you will and since not all can come forward to hold their hands, I ask that you pray with us for strength and forgiveness for these families. Let us pray."

There was a short pause.

"Dear Lord, our most merciful Father. As You've heard today, these families seek reconciliation with their fellow believers. They desire to rededicate their lives to You and live according to Your Word and Your Guidance. Lord, they acknowledge that they're sinners, and that they've made mistakes. They acknowledge that their celebrity status is nothing compared to You. They desire to cast away the ungodly actions that have caused Staci, Michael, and Celeste to be here today. Lord, I ask that You please forgive Staci, Michael, and Celeste for the transgressions that they have committed to each other, to their fellow believers, and most of all to You, our Gracious and Merciful Lord. May the members of this family before You on this stage and also to our Brothers and Sisters here in Texas, California, and elsewhere, accept their rededication of their lives to You. In the name of Jesus Christ, Your Son and our Lord…Amen!"

Justin reminded everyone that more news might appear in the future. He reminded everyone to be careful about misinformation—"fake news." He encouraged both congregations and the Web audience to use discernment when any news story might appear about Staci, Celeste, or me, in the upcoming days and weeks. Justin asked everyone to continue praying for our families.

Finally, our California brethren said goodbye to us via the Web. As Justin concluded the worship service, he announced that at this time for security reasons, our family wouldn't be able to visit with or provide autographs to the audience, because we needed to leave after the service. At some future date, we would try to provide that opportunity.

As the congregation began dispersing, the security team was on heightened alert to escort us out of the sanctuary through the way we came in. As we got back into our vehicles, some of our security entourage joined us to leave the church for our home in Plano.

As we were making the trek back, I decided to turn on the radio to hear what the news might be saying. The traffic was gradually picking up around the church. We got out before many of the members had even left the building. Once we were on the road, the hourly radio newscast finally made it to the air on my favorite DFW news station. As we continued home, a news story of shocking proportions hit. I had to pull the car over to deal with the initial shock. The news announcement revealed the following story:

"Some breaking news from this morning in Hollywood. Television producer, showrunner, former actor, and businessman Albert Jacobs is dead. The sixty-nine-year-old former executive producer and creator of the television series *'Goodwin Circle'* and the recent FibreTainment reboot series *'Goodwin Circles Around Again'* was found dead this morning in his Bel Air, California estate. His body was found approximately 8:45 a.m. Pacific Time by his housekeeping staff. A 911 call was made from the Jacobs's estate shortly after Jacobs's body was found. The LAPD were called to investigate. Paramedics were also called because one member of the housekeeping staff became distraught upon learning of Jacobs's unexpected death. Staff claimed when they left Friday night that Jacobs was last seen lounging in a recliner, smoking a cigar, and drinking while watching TV in a downstairs room where his body was later found. One person on the scene—speaking on condition of anonymity—said that the particular room reeked with the heavy smell of alcoholic beverages and cigar smoke."

"Initial reports suggest that foul play isn't likely since Jacobs's house was under twenty-four-hour private security surveillance. Jacobs's body has been sent for an autopsy. No funeral or memorial arrangements have been announced at this time. However, many accolades have been pouring in from around the country and the world. We will have more details later. Once again, television producer, and businessman Albert Jacobs is dead at sixty-nine. In other entertainment news…"

Since I stopped on the side of the road, Kyle exited the other vehicle. Celeste rolled down her passenger-side window.

I broke the news to Kyle. "Kyle, Jacobs is dead."

Kyle was in disbelief. "What?! You're kidding."

"You heard me right. We just heard on the radio. Albert Jacobs was found dead this morning at his home in Bel Air. They don't know for sure what really killed him. The police are investigating."

"I'll tell Staci and the others," said Kyle. "Are you going to be okay?"

"Other than being a little flustered, yes," I said. "It's a shock to learn this news."

"We'll see you at your house." Kyle walked back to his vehicle.

As Celeste rolled up the window, I commented, "What a shock! What a way to go!"

"Unfortunately, that happens," consoled Celeste.

"It sure does. You know what we've been warned many times…over the years?"

"'For the wages of sin is death…'"

"Yep, and the rest of that verse is, 'but the gift of God is eternal life in Christ Jesus our Lord.' *[Romans 6:23, NASB]*. I didn't hate Albert. I'm not sure if he was ever a believer."

Celeste said, "His 'fruits' sure didn't seem like it." *[Matthew 7:15-23, Matthew 12:33-37, Luke 6:43-45]*.

"It isn't our place to judge or decide," I said. "Only God knows now for sure. We can speculate, but we weren't there in Albert's last moments to know for sure."

I turned off the hazard flashers, put the gear in drive, and made our way from the shoulder to the highway. Kyle followed our lead. When we got back to the house, we had an early afternoon dinner. Around 7:00 p.m., Kyle and Staci with their kids, Mom, and Dad traveled back to Frisco. Celeste and I remained at home with our kids.

Later that evening, we watched the 10:00 p.m. news on KSFD. I was really surprised that the story made it to the evening news. We saw the news story about Albert Jacobs's death. The newscasters shared our story and footage from the church service. As we watched, they acknowledged that we were unaware of Albert Jacobs's death during the church service since that news didn't become public until that afternoon around 12:30 p.m. Central Time. They referred to our agent, Jamie, that we wouldn't be giving any comment concerning Albert Jacobs's passing at this time because of some pending litigation. However, Jamie provided the statement that, "Our hearts and prayers go to the Jacobs family." Staci, Celeste, and I didn't socialize much with Albert Jacobs over those years. It was all business. In show business, it wasn't all fun. We learned that lesson many years ago; and unfortunately, we learned an all too well-known issue when the wrong choices can eventually lead to a demise. With Albert Jacobs dead, there were no answers as to how the series would proceed, or if it would be canceled.

We visited one last time with Kyle and Staci and family at Mom and Dad's house in Frisco the next day. Kyle, Staci, and their kids flew back to California on that Tuesday. Over the next few days and weeks, we never imagined what would happen next.

11

THE AFTERMATH

◆   ◆   ◆

Over the next month, I continued my voice-over work. We learned later that the FBI had discovered two different individuals who had mailed threatening letters from different post offices around the country to Celeste's and Staci's fan mail addresses. Karl Ramirez was handling the proceedings. We wouldn't have to appear in court. The LAPD determined laundry detergent was the white powder discovered in one of Celeste's fan mail letters at PRI International's Century City Office. FBI agents, federal marshals, and U.S. Postal Inspectors were hunting for the suspects behind this particular letter. We were told they had some leads but no additional details.

By August, SYZ Studios announced that they were planning to release the season two episodes of *"Goodwin Circles Around Again."* The episodes were expected by the end of September. The kids were back in school once again. Staci had been busy with another TV movie in upstate New York. From what I could see online, fan reactions were mixed about whether there would be any additional episodes of *"Goodwin Circles Around Again"* or the show would simply fade away with no real conclusion.

By the middle of September, I was taking a short hiatus. I was at home with Celeste. She had been reviewing some potential acting jobs. At one point, Staci called Celeste to see if she could step into a role at the last minute. The original actress had become sick. Celeste flew to upstate New York for a few days to participate in Staci's latest TV movie project. Staci said the target date was for an upcoming March or April premiere on the Gold Entertainment Network. She had told me that some of the Gold Entertainment executives and producers were wondering why I wouldn't audition for some of their projects. I had thought about it, and I told them I would keep them in mind. I also had told them that I had some story ideas, and they were willing to talk further. They had reviewed my voice-over production website to see my resume and bio. Some of them remembered me from *"Goodwin Circle."*

Jamie Caballero called from Los Angeles to notify us of the plans being made for *"Goodwin Circles Around Again."* Krista Rodriguez, one of the former co-executive producers of our original show had been hired as the new showrunner and executive producer. Over the years, we had stayed in touch with Krista, because she had become a very good friend behind the scenes. Staci and Celeste were relieved that Krista had been hired, because she didn't approve of Albert Jacobs's racy storylines. Despite working with Jacobs many years ago, she was one of the control measures that Jerry Knobele insisted on, following the *"It's Our Time"* debacle. Unfortunately, she wasn't there when the reboot began. SYZ Studios, FibreTainment, and Krista had discussed what direction should the show should go at this point; Staci, Celeste, and I also discussed with them via conference call.

Celeste was completely against returning to the show for a third season. Staci didn't think she could continue the show alone. All three of us agreed that the show couldn't continue to have the dark, raunchy, and ruckus tone the first two seasons had. If you think we were being selfish in possibly ending the show, several of the new cast shared our displeasure with what had happened. After several talks, FibreTainment agreed that instead of a season three, we'd have a wrap-up TV movie. It would be a two-hour finale film to tie up all of the series' loose ends. The entire production would be a closed set with no studio audience. There was some debate if a laugh track would be used or not. Celeste agreed to return for the TV movie as long as she had some creative control. Staci also signed on with a similar stipulation as Celeste's contract. When I learned this, I suggested that I should come back and resolve the maligned storyline of Davey's off-screen cheating and Debbie's off-screen divorce. I insisted that storyline needed to be fixed. With assistance of the writers, I helped craft a portion of the concluding minutes of the movie. The expected release date was for the following spring.

Finally, *"Goodwin Circles Around Again"* Season Two premiered on FibreTainment for the world to enjoy to their hearts content, or gag to their dismay. I saw the media critics and the various fan blogger reviews. Despite a few changes in the storylines, the show fared a little better than season one. Unfortunately, the writing was on the wall. Many old fans had moved on. We learned that many Christians had been saddened and upset by the poor decisions that were made in the series' production. Christian sites and news services commented that the season two shows were still stuck in an "irreverent, disgusting tripe and rehash that no one would want to watch again." Albert Jacobs's last call was the tarnishing of his sitcom "masterpiece."

Devoted fans of the new show were saddened to learn that SYZ Studios and FiberTainment were ending the show with a special TV movie for season three. FibreTainment executives had seen what we had said at the church service earlier that summer. Many fans had watched that service as well. Justin Lockwood reported that both Spring Creek church Web sites had reported record numbers of views of that church service. The court injunction worked to prevent any firing of Celeste or Staci. SYZ Studios, FibreTainment, and Krista Rodriguez were willing to allow us to conclude the show. SYZ Studios and FibreTainment agreed to compensate some of my motivational speaker business losses, because some churches canceled for Celeste's participation on the new show.

By November, Staci was back home in California with her family. Celeste flew to California to begin shooting the TV movie finale of *"Goodwin Circles Around Again."* Mom, Dad, and the kids flew out to California with me. I had to film some of my scenes for the show. With the Thanksgiving holiday approaching that year, it made more sense to celebrate the holiday in California. By mid-December, we finished the final scenes of this TV movie. It seemed strange to be back on the same soundstage where we had taped our show many years ago. Being on that living room set again brought back some wonderful memories. I learned that it wasn't the original set because SYZ Studios had allowed the permanent destruction of the old sets. Some parts went on to other productions, while others were eventually tossed on the scrap heap. We spent a few weeks creating that final TV movie to wrap up all of the storylines.

December finally arrived. We had Christmas back in Plano and Frisco. Staci, Kyle, and their kids were back. We spent many evenings either going into Dallas or other communities to see various festivities or going back and forth between our family homes in Plano and Frisco. We even watched a few of Staci's Christmas movies from the past few years. Christmas and New Years went by so quickly that Staci and her family were back in California in no time.

My motivational speaking business rebounded that fall and winter, and into the spring. Jamie Caballero said that many churches had requested to see our June church service again because it was one of the most heartfelt experiences they had ever seen. Several TV friends sent notices that clips of our church service and testimonies had traveled to other parts of the world. Many had shared their condolences for the trouble we had experienced, and many had asked for reconciliation. As churches were contacting us to schedule a time to visit, one particular church in the Memphis, Tennessee metro area had requested a date in late January. Weather could always be unpredictable in the winter months in the south. This church had requested if Staci could attend. We called Staci to see if she would be available to meet us in Memphis and attend this special event. Fortunately, Staci's schedule was open that particular weekend. Kyle had to stay home because he was working on a business proposal. He also needed to stay close to the kids, Alex and Amy. We arranged our flights where Staci would fly directly to Memphis from LAX. We did the same from DFW to Memphis, at close to the same time.

We arranged for a security company to chauffeur us to and from the Memphis airport and elsewhere around town. We didn't make a big announcement on local media that we would be in the area. Instead, we simply announced on social media and our websites that we would be having a motivational speaking event at a local Cordova church. There was something special about this church. While we were making our way to our hotel, it suddenly hit me. This church was the home church of the mother whose daughter had died in that fraternity party accident, months earlier. I reminded Celeste and Staci when I realized this. I was surprised the church pastor hadn't said anything.

We settled in our hotel and contacted the church pastor that we had arrived. We would visit with him the next day to finalize what we planned to do the next two nights. While in our conversation, he brought to my attention about the mother we had only spoken with by phone. The pastor told us the mother had requested that we try to visit her home after one of the speaking events.

"You want us to do what?" I asked.

"Yes, we would like you, Celeste, and Staci to visit the home of Mrs. Denise Smith after one of the speaking nights."

"We don't usually do that…"

"In this case, we request you should. I deeply request you should. I could try to tell you why. I think this situation would be much better that you go and see for yourself."

"What will we see?" I inquired because I was very curious. "Why not just tell us?"

"Trust me," said the pastor. "You have to see this at her home to understand. You'll not be alone. Your driver and I will be there."

"You can't just tell us?"

"Ms. Denise is a very sweet lady, a God-fearing, Christ-loving example of a Christian despite all that she has lived through, especially these last few years."

"It's that important?" I asked.

"Mike, I believe that Ms. Denise would be a wonderful example for y'all to meet."

"We'll visit Denise at her home on the last night."

During some of our time in the Memphis area, I recommended we visit at least one or two barbecue joints. Memphis barbecue is different in style, taste, and flavor from Texas barbecue. I always enjoyed getting to see different parts of the country, seeing some sights, meeting people, and trying some of the local cuisine.

During the first speaking night, we met Denise. She was very nice. She told us that she was one of our biggest fans. She had forgotten to tell us that months ago when we visited by phone. Since she was in high school, she was a fan of our original show. It was through her that her late daughter had also become a fan.

We arranged to visit Denise's home in Collierville after our second night's program. It was a little bit of a drive from the hotel to the church. Fortunately, we had local drivers who knew the areas much better than we did. We finished our second night's program around 8:30 p.m. Several people wanted to visit afterward, and we tried to accommodate as best we could. The church pastor called to tell Denise that we would be running a little late. She said that she still wanted us to visit.

By 9:30 p.m., we were back in the chauffeured car. We were on our way to Denise's home in Collierville. When we arrived, we found ourselves in a typical American subdivision of modest but nice homes. Most of the houses appeared to be one-story, modern wood frame with at least three bedrooms. A few were two-story homes. While some had brick, others had a variety of exterior surfaces.

Denise's home was a one-story house with a car parked in the attached carport. A floodlight illuminated the carport, and I assumed this was for security reasons. Our driver had parked in front of the house. While the driver stayed with the car, all three of us—Staci, Celeste, and I—exited the car and stepped into Denise's front yard.

We also noticed another car was parked in the driveway but not under the carport. We learned that was the church pastor's car, when he and Denise greeted us inside. Denise offered us some cookies and coffee. Staci and Celeste accepted water. Now that we were there, the big question was about to be answered.

"Ms. Smith, you asked us to come visit you at your home," I said.

"Yes. I told you that I've been a fan of all three of you since I was in high school," said Denise. "About midway through college, we had my daughter. My late husband and I raised her until he died."

"What happened?"

"Combat-related. He was on patrol in Iraq back in 2003. He drove his Jeep over a hidden IED. They told me that he didn't know what hit him."

I walked across the living room and noticed the folded U.S. American flag in a glass case, a plaque honoring his service, and a color photograph of the deceased husband/father in uniform.

"We're sorry to hear about this. We thank you for your husband's honorable service to our country," consoled Staci.

"There were many days that went by that I prayed and hoped for a safe return. After that fateful day..." Denise closed her eyes and shed a few tears.

"Denise, that's okay," comforted the pastor. "He was an honorable man, businessman, soldier, and most of all a believer."

"Is this what you wanted us to see?" I compassionately asked the pastor.

"What she wanted you to see is in a bedroom."

Celeste and I proceed to learn what was so special about this bedroom. The pastor turned on a hallway light and told us that the second door on the right was the daughter's bedroom. The door was closed. He said that a light switch could be found on the wall on the left side of the door as we walked in. When I opened the bedroom door and flicked on the switch, the light displayed a typical young woman's bedroom. Staci had stayed with Denise to help comfort her. Celeste and I looked around. Twin-sized bed, end table and bedroom lamp, dresser, school desk and chair, posters of all sorts on the wall, and a couple of bookcases in two different parts of the room. We also saw a hinged-folding set of closet doors at one end of the room.

As Celeste and I looked around, something caught Celeste's eye. "You need to look over here at this bookcase by the dresser. I think this is what they are wanting us to see."

Back in the living room, Denise had regained her composure. She was smiling again. Celeste and I had left the bedroom. We made our way back to the living room where the pastor, Denise, and Staci were visiting.

As I approached, I said, "Staci, the bookcase by the dresser. That's what you want to look at...what's on the three middle shelves."

"Can you just tell me?"

"As the pastor said, you have to see it."

"Should I go alone? You look like you and Celeste have been crying."

"You'll understand why." My tone was somber. "You have to see it for yourself; however, I'll be outside the door."

Staci looked at me, then at Celeste, then at the pastor, and then finally at Denise—seeming bewildered. She had traveled the farthest of all of us to be there. Now, she was visiting the home of a college student who had died in Memphis many months earlier as a result of a college fraternity party stunt gone wrong. That stunt was based on a crazy scene from the first season, fourth episode of that show that Staci had starred in.

"I'll be right behind you," as I hinted to her to brace herself for what she was about to see back there.

Staci looked at me. Then, she closed her eyes. She seemed to be praying softly to herself. I couldn't understand what she was saying. Then, she opened her eyes.

"Pardon me, Mrs. Smith, I must see what you've asked me to see."

Staci got up and walked to the girl's bedroom. As I caught up with her, she was looking around the room. I peeked just enough to see her become fixated on the particular bookcase. When she looked up, she gasped, widened her eyes, and placed her hands over her mouth. I could tell that she was looking at the upper left side of the second shelf from the top.

On the left side of that shelf was a mint condition *"Goodwin Circle"* school metal lunchbox. These were popular in the 1980s. I was told that this one also had—in mint condition—its original insulated thermos. Toward the middle, there were two mint condition *"Goodwin Circle"* coloring books enclosed in special plastic protectors like one would use for comic books. There were even a few television program guides—some local and some national—that showed us on the cover at different times over the years. The right side of the shelf were six paperback books labeled *"Goodwin Circle"* book series. I vaguely recall that book series. Some writers licensed the show's name and characters. These were stories that were more than a typical thirty-minute sitcom plot. I think one of them was a mystery wherein Robin and Davey played detective sleuths.

As Staci lowered her eyes to the next shelf, she saw four black-and-white photographs in standing picture frames. Each photograph was a celebrity headshot of four very familiar people. Each photo was from a set taken around 2002 for the upcoming, second, and final *"Goodwin Circle"* movie.

The far right one had written in the lower left of the picture, "To Our Sister in Christ, Rachel. Love, Celeste Hernandez-Whitman." On the next one was written in the lower left of the picture, "To Our Sister in Christ, Rachel. Love, Mike Whitman." On the next picture, "To Our Sister in Christ, Rachel. Love, Kyle Carella." On the last photo was written in the lower right of the picture, "To Our Sister in Christ, Rachel. Love, Staci Whitman-Carella." All were written in cursive and permanent marker.

Staci then noticed the small photo book on the shelf in front of the headshot photos. She opened it and saw more photos. They were color photos from a day that all four of us participated many years ago in Memphis. When I had glanced at the photos, I was able to pinpoint roughly when and why we were there. The Memphis affiliate of the ASC Network WTSV was one of our "whistle-stop" tours to promote our very last TV movie around the country. We met our fans, signed autographs, and did all sorts of local promotional stuff.

Every photo in the book had at least one of us with what appeared to be a six- or seven-year-old little girl. One photo had all four of us with the little girl. Some of the photos also included pictures of Denise with each one of us. Staci sniffed and teared up as she looked through the book, as I watched from a distance. When I looked at the photos, I was able to determine this was a promotion event that had been held at the Wolfchase Galleria, a shopping mall in the Memphis area. Many of the photos were taken in front of a backdrop that included multiple company logos: WTSV, the ASC Network, a couple of Memphis radio stations, and one of the department stores in the mall, with the Wolfchase Galleria being the main sponsor.

Staci finally broke loose and exclaimed, "Michael! Michael! Michael!"

I quickly entered the bedroom. She turned to me and buried her head into my shoulder.

"It's ok," as I held Staci. "Now we know why they wanted us to see this," as I shed more tears about our discovery.

Staci looked up, trying to talk through her tears. "She was one of our fans!"

"I know," I responded, fighting back my own tears. "And now, I seem to vaguely remember that little girl all over again. Her father had died in Iraq that year while serving with our nation's troops. Our visit on that summer day at the Wolfchase Galleria was a very special one."

Celeste and the pastor came back to the room. Denise followed.

I turned to Denise and the pastor. "We've seen what you wanted us to see. Thank you."

"Denise and her daughter met us years ago in Memphis at that shopping mall," reminded Celeste.

"Yep," I admitted, "and that was over ten years ago."

"Nearly fifteen years ago," commented Celeste.

"I bought that lunch box while I was in high school," shared Denise. "I never used it. I couldn't bring myself to put lunch in it and carry it every day. It was a kid's lunch box, and I wasn't the kid I thought. I just thought it might make a good collector's item. I enjoyed your first show a lot."

We all smiled. However, Denise seemed to understand why Staci, Celeste, and I smiling through our tears.

"I couldn't understand why in the second show they had to put all of that disgusting and vulgar content," shared Denise.

"I'm sorry that Celeste and I were involved in that," expressed Staci. "We were taken advantage of."

"Yes," admitted Celeste, "I'm sorry we said those awful words and behaved as we did."

"Even though it was acting," continued Staci, "it still was wrong. I wish that we could do something. "

"My daughter was pursuing theatre arts as a minor with her math teaching degree," shared Denise.

"We can think of some ideas, but it's getting late. Celeste, Staci, and I have to get some sleep to make our flights tomorrow. We appreciate your hospitality," I thanked Denise.

"Sure. Anytime," said Denise. "I don't hold any of you responsible. Y'all shared what happened with your church and the whole world. I've forgiven y'all. I forgive you again."

Denise stepped forward to hug each one of us.

"I hope the special TV movie will make up for some of the terrible wrongs," said Celeste.

"I hope so, too," said Denise. "Kids these days don't need more trashy storylines and filth on TV. There's enough happening everyday out there...elsewhere...and much worse in 'real life!'"

"Unfortunately, Celeste and I helped contribute to the problem," Staci admitted.

"God is goin' to make right," assured Denise. "He knows y'all didn't mean to cause this."

Staci frowned, still seeming ashamed.

"Don't be ashamed. You're believers. We're believers. Christ is with us. He knows," assured Denise.

"You're so right, Ms. Denise," said the pastor, "Romans 8:28-39."

Denise and the pastor made their way back to the hallway and eventually the living room. We took another moment to review the pictures and take in what one of our devoted fans had kept all of these years.

I peeked in the closet. Many of the daughter's extra clothes were still hanging. I even saw some boots and shoes. As I was examining the bedroom closet, Celeste called to me.

"Michael," scolded Celeste, "why are you snooping in there?"

"I'm not sure why," I admitted.

"That's rude to be peering into the young woman's closet like that!" retorted Celeste.

"Denise hasn't removed all of her daughter's items."

"Michael, do you have any respect for a mother to have time to mourn?"

"Sorry, it was just an observation. We know that young girl was loved by her family and her church."

"It was a tragic accident that took her," said Celeste. "Someone at the college pushed her into that accident."

"She didn't deserve to have that happen to her. She had her whole life ahead of her."

Celeste assured, "Despite what led to this accident, we know she was a believer. She didn't normally drink, from what I was told about her. Someone took advantage of the situation."

"Taking advantage of someone...a believer. That sounds familiar." I looked at Celeste and Staci who didn't answer. They understood through their expressions.

After a few minutes, the three of us left the bedroom and walked back to the living room. Before we left, the pastor asked that we pray. He asked for healing and reconciling to continue with Denise and all of our families. He also prayed that our devoted fans, who were hurt by the first two seasons of *"Goodwin Circles Around Again"*— especially our Christian fans, would continue to join us in reconciling for the problems that the reboot series had brought. Finally, he prayed for a safe journey and future success for Staci, Celeste, and me.

12

THE CONCLUSION

◆————◆————◆

After meeting Denise, we arrived at the hotel rather late. When we got up the next morning, we prepared for our journey home. Our security bodyguard was ready as well. Our chauffeured ride arrived at the hotel for our eventual trip to the airport. Before heading for the airport, I asked the driver to take us to a cemetery in Collierville. The pastor gave me the address and where to find the young girl's marked grave.

After a few minutes driving, we arrived at the cemetery and pulled as close to the girl's gravesite as we could within the marked driveways. We found that someone had recently placed a small wreath of flowers at the grave. Although the day was sunny, the air was rather chilly for this partly sunny west Tennessee day. I removed from my pocket a promotional *"Goodwin Circle"* button and pinned it onto the existing wreath. We wanted to show our respects to this young girl we briefly met years ago and unfortunately, whose death came too soon. After some reflection and thoughts, we prayed a short prayer to honor her memory. The three of us believed that the young girl was completely unaware that she was in danger at the time; unfortunately by the time she was intoxicated, we believed she was unable to decide for herself. After our prayer, I suggested that we needed to leave.

As we jumped into the chauffeured car, the driver discovered a problem. The car wouldn't start.

"That doesn't sound good," said Staci.

Our driver commented, "I don't know if it's the battery or the alternator."

Our bodyguard got out with the driver to look under the hood. Our bodyguard quipped, "I hope it's not the starter."

Our driver and the bodyguard got back in the car.

"Whatever it is, we aren't going anywhere," declared our driver. "I'll call our roadside personnel. They'll be here in a few minutes."

"That could take longer than usual," I commented. "That's been my experience with roadside assistance the last few times I've used them."

"Our roadside assistance is in-house and in this area," assured our driver. "They should be here soon."

"We might be cutting it too close to get to the airport," fretted Celeste. "Our flight will be arriving soon."

"It's a charter. At least we can all fly on the same flight to Dallas," shared Staci.

Our driver got a text message on his phone "Oh, great. Our roadside folks are going to be a while."

"Maybe we can call for a SHAR'D ride," I suggested. "If we do, maybe their driver can help you give this car a jump start, so you can get to a mechanic or back to your company's garage to look at it."

"If you're in a hurry to get to the airport, you may need to do that," said our driver. "It could take up to forty-five minutes to get our roadside assistance here."

"I don't mind calling for a SHAR'D," I approved.

SHAR'D was one of those private taxi services that uses a phone app to request and pay for rides. I had to use a SHAR'D a couple of times when a private limo or chauffeured-ride service wasn't available. I requested an SUV ride. Within ten minutes, an SUV pulled into the cemetery. The SHAR'D driver texted and then called, needing help to find us.

"Are any of you, Mike?" asked the SHAR'D driver from his window.

"I'm Mike," I said from our back window. "Our ride is having battery or alternator trouble, we think. If it's only battery trouble, the driver needs a jump start. We need to get to the airport to catch a flight."

"By the way, my name is Paul."

"Nice to meet you, Paul," I greeted. Paul and his vehicle description matched on the app.

"Let me see if I have my jumper cables," offered Paul. "I'll be glad to give y'all some help. If it's just the battery, I may be able to get your car started. If not, you may have to wait for your roadside folks."

Paul turned his car to align the front of his SUV with our driver's vehicle. Since our driver had already popped open the hood, Paul wasted no time stopping his SUV, popping the hood, and running to the back to find his set of jumper cables in the cargo hold. The SHAR'D driver returned to the front of his car with the jumper cables. Our driver and Paul attached the jumper cables to the battery terminals, then, both drivers reentered their respective vehicles. Paul started first. Then, our driver followed. Our driver's car struggled a little but finally started.

Paul said, "I'm glad to help."

Our driver popped open the trunk. We retrieved our baggage and made our way to Paul's SUV.

As we were making our way to Paul's vehicle, I had to quip, "Staci! Wearing an outfit like that, folks are going to think that you SHAR'D more than a ride!"

Staci scowled, "You silly!"

"Wait a minute! You've heard that joke?!" exclaimed Paul.

I began, "Yes, and—"

"Corporate has told us to tell everyone to stop telling that joke," cautioned Paul. "They don't like it, and they don't appreciate that TV show for creating it. It's become a big joke for customers to insult our drivers with. I've forgotten the particular show's name, but it was vulgar. Corporate wants no association with it."

"Okay," I apologized. "I understand. I'll never say it again."

"Thank you," cautioned Paul. "Please tell others to stop making that joke to our drivers and service."

As we loaded our bags into the vehicle, our bodyguard who was riding with us joined us in the SHAR'D SUV. As we were getting ready to leave, our original chauffeur driver motioned to Paul to come over to talk for a moment.

Staci, Celeste, and I were all seated in the back. Our bodyguard sat in the front passenger seat. Paul made his way back to the SUV, opened his side door, and climbed in. We watched and waved as our original chauffeur's vehicle slowly pulled away.

"You're heading for the Memphis Airport?" asked Paul.

"Close to it," I said. "We're flying out on a charter flight. It's supposed to arrive by 1:30 p.m. We need to get there as soon as possible. We don't wanna be late."

"Completely understand," as Paul started the car and began driving.

Paul acknowledged the charter flight service's address, which we requested, on the SHAR'D Driver phone app. As we talked with Paul, he started some chitchat, asking about where we were from. He started with our bodyguard, Jake. Jake told him that he was from around the Memphis area. He was simply a security detail for hire. The chauffeur service was part of his employment as a bodyguard.

"So, what about the three of you? Are you from Memphis in some way?"

"My wife, Celeste, and I are from the Dallas metro area," I answered as Celeste waved her hand.

"I'm originally from the Dallas area as well, but home is elsewhere," piped Staci.

Paul asked, "Where's home for you?"

Staci answered, "West Coast."

"Wow! Where on the West Coast?"

"California."

"Any particular place?"

"California is all I'll say."

"You sure want to be vague about where you're from?"

"She likes her privacy," I smirked.

"I see," said Paul.

Paul turned to Jake. "Jake, do these folks have something special about them that they need to hire you to chauffeur them around?"

"I just do what I'm hired to do," answered Jake. "I'm a bodyguard."

Paul asked us, "Do y'all do anything special as a job?"

"Various things," I said.

"Celeste?"

"I've done some acting."

"Okay, how about Ms. Staci?"

"I'm in between jobs at the moment. I've done similar work."

I could tell that Staci and Celeste didn't want to let on to their identities. At some point, he was going to figure it out. I just knew that the SHAR'D joke could've raised some suspicions. I decided to play it cool and ask about the company's stance on it.

"So what was this issue with the joke that I said earlier?" I asked Paul.

"As I explained, I received orders from corporate to tell riders to stop saying that joke."

"What led to those orders?"

"The CEO is a family man. He has three kids of his own—three young kids at that! When he learned that this TV show had mentioned SHAR'D in a joke, it made him wonder 'Why did the writers do that?' Then, he tuned into the show."

"He didn't like it?"

"To put it mildly. He didn't like the 'clever' joke about SHAR'D."

"Not so clever," commented Staci.

"To suggest our drivers might do something inappropriate with a client," condemned Paul. "It's against company policy anyway."

"I'm glad to know about your company policy," I reassured.

Paul continued, "He said the actress who said the joke should've known better than to go along with it. Word has it that the actress relished saying it."

The joke had been a punchline in a *"Goodwin Circles Around Again"* Season One episode. I can't remember which one. It had become a popular joke among fans. Celeste, as Debbie, wore a rather revealing outfit in that scene. It was Staci, as Robin, who recited the SHAR'D service punchline for the camera.

"The CEO really cares about his kids. He was very shocked how that TV show was done," said Paul. "That joke really made him mad. He threatened to pursue legal action."

I looked at Staci.

"Where did you hear this?" I asked.

Paul answered, "He talked about it in a shareholder meeting sometime back. He was very torn by seeing that behavior exhibited by the actress, who called herself a Christian."

"I see…" as I looked at Staci.

"If he had the chance, he said he would like to tell that young lady what he thought—not only for the SHAR'D joke but also about being a Christian."

"Did he say anything else? He has to realize that those actors were following a script…"

"He said that he would like her to know that our drivers and riders aren't allowed to do any 'inappropriate stuff,' inside or outside the vehicle. I think he'd also request an apology from her for telling the joke. I'm surprised that the show and its…its…company…"

"Studio?" I implied.

"Yeah," answered Paul, "studio and channel haven't been sued yet."

Celeste sighed, "Dear Precious Lord…"

Paul continued, "Since the controversy that spawned all over that show, I'm not surprised. At least the three actors finally admitted they weren't behind the jokes and content. It still hurts…"

"I think we understand," I admitted.

"You think…you might understand?" asked Paul.

I nodded.

"Wait a minute, I think I know where I've seen all three of you."

Staci, Celeste, and I looked at each other. I had a hunch that Paul knew who we were. He was waiting until the right moment to tell us. We waited a few minutes to say anything else to Paul. I decided to see if Paul would determine our identities from discussing the TV shows.

"Paul, can I assume that you watch TV?"

"Yes."

"Anything particular?"

"Football, basketball, baseball, and the news. I also watch some reality TV and documentaries."

"Any sitcoms?"

"Mostly classic stuff when I do. Many sitcoms that they air today are nothing compared to yesteryear."

"What old sitcoms do you watch?"

Paul started to list a bunch of 1950s through 1980s shows. I had heard of many of them. I even recall watching a few. Staci, Celeste, and I had met or knew some of the actors and actresses who brought those shows to life.

"I remember this one called *Godwin's Circle*...I think that's what it was called. Really fun show."

"You mean *Goodwin's Circle*?"

"That was it. Really funny show. Watched it a lot growing up and later in reruns. I didn't watch too many of the other sitcoms by the late '80s and into the '90s. *'Goodwin Circle'* was a classic show to watch on Friday nights back in the day!"

"That's interesting," I said. "All three of us remember that show."

"Are you fans?"

I turned, smiled to Celeste. "You could say that."

Paul replied, "I don't remember all of the episodes. It was on for a long time."

"So I have heard as well," commented Staci.

"Then, they had to go do this new show where they changed up the parents and did a bunch of crazy stuff," remarked Paul. "It was a real shame to see what they did to the new show."

"Was this the same show that had the joke?" I asked.

"Yeah. The new show was centering on the former kids and their perverted families. A lot of bad stuff presented."

"I'm sorry to hear that."

"My company's CEO isn't surprised that they're ending production."

"They *have* ended production. There's one final TV movie to wrap up the loose ends coming in September."

"I don't know if I'll watch it. The shows they released the first year were just...awful."

"Awful?" asked Celeste.

"Lots of sex references, profane language, sex jokes, etc.," commented Paul. "Not for the young kids for sure."

"TV sure has changed." I turned, looking at Staci.

"This one wasn't even on regular TV," said Paul. "This one was on a streamed service."

"Was there anything else wrong with it?" asked Staci.

"That girl named…Robin?" remarked Paul. "I think that's her name. She really turned out terrible. Not a good person at all."

"The actress may not be that way in real life," noted Staci.

"That might be true," admitted Paul. "Unfortunately, the content of the show and some of the acting left a lot to be desired. Too much emphasis on alcohol. That frat party episode was unwatchable…and inexcusable. I heard that a Collierville girl, a local girl, died last year at an in-state college…in a real frat party that was inspired by one on the show!"

"The first year, fourth episode?" I asked.

"Yeah," Paul disgusted. "Total disregard for the viewers; especially for the parents with young children. It was borderline…not exactly know how to describe it."

"That's really a shame," I said, dismayed.

"I'd say," agreed Paul.

I decided that it was time to tell Paul the truth. I suspected he knew who we were. I thought this might be the chance for Paul to tell Staci directly.

"Paul, what'd you say if I told you that the young lady that you dislike for saying that SHAR'D joke is seated behind you?"

"Really?"

Staci looked at me and stuck her tongue at me briefly.

Paul scolded, "I saw that!"

Staci turned forward, looking stunned and then looked back at me.

"You aren't fooling me," said Paul. "I had a clue who you were."

"I'm sorry that I caused so much trouble," apologized Staci. "I shouldn't have stuck my tongue at you, Mike. That was unkind of me."

"Brothers and sisters have their moments," admitted Paul, "even as adults."

"I don't usually behave like that with Celeste around," answered Staci. "I guess I slipped up."

Paul shared, "I've read and seen everything that I could see concerning what happened to *'Goodwin Circles Around Again'* and the cancelation. I've been a fan since the original show's premiere back in 1988. I just wanted to see if you'd do anything to admit to it or say something first."

"If you've seen and read just about everything, I guess you heard about our Sunday public confession months ago," I shared.

"Heard about it? I saw it! I watched it online and watched it again! News broke around the country about it! All of the entertainment shows grabbed footage about it! They'd never seen anything like it, ever! I had to go watch the entire special church service just to see all of what each of you said! I'd never seen anything like that! I saw the whole service...more than once. Fellow fans, who were upset by the first season first episode, were so relieved that all three of you came forward. Some of my friends were wondering if you were heading down the same path as a bunch of those other Hollywood types."

"Unfortunately, Hollywood has had its share of successes and failures," I commented.

"Celeste and I have never had a whole series considered a failure," shared Staci.

"Staci, believe me. Failure can be only one bump in the road," Paul explained. "When it happens, it seems like the whole world is against you and that God has forsaken you. It's not that way. God is still there with you *[Romans 8:31, 1 Kings 8:57, Psalms 118:6, Isaiah 41:10, Jeremiah 20:11, Jeremiah 42:11, 1 John 4:4]*. God can take that failure or loss and turn it toward something good *[Deuteronomy 23:5, Romans 8:28, Isaiah 61:1-11, The Book of Job]*, despite the cancelation of this new show. Your public confession made it clear that you weren't in control of all of your actions."

"I guess it was really that bad," said Staci.

"Staci, I had some friends who liked the show—maybe a dozen friends. Four of them were women," continued Paul. "One lady was disheartened because she wouldn't be able to let her kids watch this show. Most of the guys hated it. They said the show played like a 'really bad chick flick' that was a total mess. The writers should've stayed with the family-friendly content. As far as the TV rating, that was very confusing for parents. You made a lot of Christians think you betrayed them. I was shocked."

"One of my friends told me that God wasn't going to allow that show to prevail without some problems, if there were any devout Christians involved. The world may have thought it was a hit, but God said 'Wait a minute! You're not putting any of My children through this mess without a fight. I'll show y'all who's boss. I'll make sure My children will see through this and not accept the ungodly un-Christian worldview that y'all tried to get one of My own to portray' *[Psalms 21:1-13, NASB paraphrased]*. Staci, I see that you learned that lesson."

"We all learned a very difficult lesson," admitted Celeste. "We just finished—before Christmas—a TV movie that will wrap up the current series."

"Celeste, is it going to be 'dark' like the new series?" asked Paul.

"This movie doesn't have Albert Jacobs's involvement."

"Albert Jacobs?"

"He created and executive-produced *'Goodwin Circle'* and *'Goodwin Circles Around Again.'* He's the one who was fired and later died."

"It's a real shame that they had to go mess up that show. I mean. The original show had such a wholesome family feel."

"Jacobs didn't think it would sell in today's television market," I said.

Paul said, "Really? I'm not surprised."

"I learned from my agent that investigators found some interesting information at Jacobs's home," I said.

"What'd they find?" asked Paul.

"They found the actual results of the test audiences that were used for the two pilots of *'Goodwin Circles Around Again.'*"

"You haven't told us about this!" said Celeste.

"What did they find?!" asked Staci.

"I just learned about this," I replied. "While investigators were going through papers found at his estate, they discovered the test audience results for the two pilots had...been...*switched*! Jacobs paid money to the testing company under the table, so to speak, to falsify the results so he could argue to take the show in the darker and sinful direction!"

"Oh, Dear Precious Lord!" Staci said. "You're saying that the first pilot was actually a winner?!"

"The first pilot actually scored an eighty-nine percent favorable rating! The second pilot received a forty-two percent favorable rating," I revealed.

"Oh no!" moaned Celeste.

Paul shook his head. "Is that amazing or what?!"

I continued, "The first pilot was family-friendly and a winner; the second pilot wasn't! Jacobs had the results switched to fool the studio and FibreTainment brass!"

"What the studio executives saw were the switched numbers and the falsified reports? Jacobs was able to convince them to take the second pilot in the darker direction. But, why?" asked Staci.

"That's apparently what happened," I said. "There was also some evidence found to corroborate the under-the-table payment with the testing company."

"This Jacobs guy found someone on the inside, and he was able to pay someone off to get the results he wanted?" asked Paul.

"That's what some additional evidence showed."

"Is that something or what? It's a total shame that one man's actions led to all of this disappointment and the possible tarnishing of your careers!"

"That is a risk that has now become apparent," admitted Staci. "As Mike has said, Hollywood isn't the same as it once was when the three of us were kids."

"I suspect that it had its danger zones back then. Think about it. Films during the Hays Code years and TV shows during the N-A-B. Television Code called for stricter standards."

I explained to Paul about the history of the Hays Code, the National Association of Broadcasters (NAB) Radio Code, and the Television Code. I shared how those codes were eventually abolished by freedom of speech arguments and foreign competition that had changed the entertainment industry.

"It's just a shame that the three of you got mixed up in that whole mess with this new show," lamented Paul.

"I wasn't directly in this mess," I acknowledged. "Guilt by association and a separate unrelated issue caused some problems for me. However, all of that is settled now."

"Staci, you won't go and do this awful stuff on your future projects?" asked Paul.

"No sir! Gold Entertainment, who produces and contracts out the movies that I star in, will never allow that stuff to happen. I'll guarantee it."

"They have a very solid code of ethics for their programs," I assured. "If they ever let go of that, that network is going to hit the skids."

"At least there's still some places of light in Hollywood," gleamed Paul.

Staci assured, "There are some Christians there, truly Bible-believing Christians. They're only human, and still susceptible to sin. Only Christ can protect them; if they truly accept and follow Him. *[Ephesians 2:8-10].*"

Celeste disclosed, "We have to be more careful next time to not let this situation happen again."

"Looks like you have your work cut out for yourselves," said Paul.

"There are many who are working to change things," I conferred. "Unfortunately, we live in a fallen world. Until Christ's return, there'll always be the temptation by some to go the ungodly way. *[Romans 5:12-14, Revelation 21:4].*"

"You've got that right!" proclaimed Paul.

We continued to our charter flight near the Memphis airport. When we arrived, I asked Paul for his contact information and what he would like on the autographed photos. I told him I would arrange for the photos to be sent soon.

Our flight arrived. They were prepared to get us first to Dallas, and eventually Staci to Los Angeles. After a few minutes of preflight checks, we were airborne.

As we flew to Dallas, we reminisced about the good times that Staci and I had growing up as kids. I reminded both of them of that special episode where I first met Celeste. Within an hour and a half, we were landing in Dallas. Celeste and I both hugged Staci. She would remain on the plane as we exited. The departing group of passengers began unloading. Celeste and I rolled our luggage off the plane. The driving service was on time to take us home. I was so happy to see home. The kids stayed with Mom and Dad that evening after we arrived home. We got a very good night's sleep that night.

Winter finally gave way to spring. North Texas was showing warmer and longer days. The premiere of the *"Goodwin Circle"* TV movie series finale finally arrived. Its premiere date had been moved to the spring. The three of us chose to keep it quiet with no major fanfare. Staci and her family flew back to Plano so we could all watch the ending together. Mom and Dad drove over from Frisco. Although most of us had seen parts of the movie get made, it was the final minutes that Staci, Kyle, Celeste, and I wanted to keep secret from the rest of the family. As everyone gathered in our living room, we announced the World Premiere of *"Goodwin Circle: Returning Home."* We activated the FibreTainment app and selected the TV movie that had become active earlier that morning.

The movie picked up shortly after the last season two episode. This time, none of the dirty language or crude images were present. As we watched, the time came where my character Davey Goodwin would finally appear at his parents' home for the first time since 1998. I remember taping these scenes. The kids laughed at my appearance. I had to grow a short beard a few days before taping to make it look like I hadn't shaven in a while. My hair was reshaped to look in tatters and more gray than I actually had. They had me wear a dark sport coat that had a few minor holes. The dark slacks had a few odd color patches and a few badly sewn rips. Davey Goodwin looked like he had seen much better days. He was also holding a beat-up hat with a hole in the center of its top. One part of my scene was with Celeste, who was playing my now on-screen ex-wife Debbie. Staci was also there as Robin.

Here's how the last parts of the movie unfolded:

"So what do you have to say for yourself, Davey?" asked Celeste.

I replied, "Debbie…I know now…I did wrong."

"You should know better!"

"But I've changed. I messed everything up. I want to make it right with everyone; including you...and fix our marriage."

"She has been through a lot, Davey!" Staci scolded.

"Robin, I really messed up for you as well. Your best friend—who I ended up marrying so long ago...and now I..."

"Look you two," cautioned Staci, "it's going to take time to mend fences."

"I have mended one fence," I answered. "I've turned my life over to Christ."

"To Jesus?" asked Celeste.

"Yes. You've always loved me. Unfortunately, I had to make that stupid mistake by cheating on you."

"Oh, Davey," Celeste whined. "It'll take time. If Robin is willing to give you that chance, I should at least try to work this out. Besides, you said you've accepted Christ."

"Yes, I have," I answered.

Celeste walked up to me and coughed. Looking disgusted, she said, "What's that smell?"

"I haven't had a bath in days."

"I'm surprised that you didn't notice it until now!" quipped Staci. "He's been a 'stinker' for a while... even while married to you!"

Celeste looked concerned and compassionate. "So you've been roughing it these last several months?"

"My clothes and hair wouldn't be this way if I was living like"—I paused—"when we were together."

Celeste conceded, "I'll take my chances and hug you. We need to work this out. You're going to need a bath...actually we both will...after this."

Celeste proceeded to hug me while we were standing in front of the living room couch. Then, the scene drastically changed. I started to cough and grasp my chest.

"What is it?!" shouted Celeste.

"Oh no!" I coughed again. "I don't know...my chest hurts..."

Suddenly, I dropped back onto the living room couch. Celeste and Staci started screaming and yelling. Celeste was pounding on my chest. It looked like a pounding, but she was playacting. I barely felt any pressure.

The screen image started to waver, wobble, and blur. When the kids first saw this, they laughed. They said they immediately realized what we had done.

The next scene blurred into place as the former scene faded. Once the next scene sharpened, we could see a bed in a typical bedroom. This set was Debbie and Davey's bedroom at their home. Celeste was lying on the bed's side toward audience right. The camera view was looking toward the front of the bed. Celeste appeared to be tossing and turning and groaning like she was having a nightmare. After a few seconds, she raised up and opened her eyes, like Debbie was unsure where she was. She appeared to be getting her bearings by looking around and finally noticing that she was in pajamas.

Celeste exclaimed, "I'm back home! In the bedroom. At our old house. Our house before."

Celeste looked and noticed a pair of men's pajamas were lying on the stage left side of the bed. Celeste reached for and took a whiff of the pajama shirt. She seemed puzzled, suggesting that something was familiar about the shirt.

This was Davey and Debbie's master bedroom. There was a master bathroom through a door farther stage left. The sound-effect folks cued the sounds of a bathtub turning on and then a shower. Celeste got up from the bed and walked to the master bathroom door. The shot changed to the second camera when Celeste entered the bathroom. She continued to hear the shower running and someone humming. I added the humming to let the viewers know that someone very familiar was there. The set designers had created a full realistic-looking master bathroom. However, the shower was mostly incomplete—which is something the viewers didn't get to see. The camera kept the shot perpendicular to the shower so the viewers wouldn't be able to see me.

After opening the curtain, Celeste widened her eyes and exclaimed, "Davey!"

The next part of the scene had Celeste jump into the shower and past the partially opened curtain. We and the viewers could hear my voice saying things like "Hey! Hey! Stop!" Celeste's voice was, "Davey! Davey! I love you!" In the process, our silliness led to the shower curtain and rod falling down. I had grabbed and shook the curtain to suggest that Debbie was so happy to find that the whole new show had been a nightmare and that Davey was very much alive. When the shower curtain and rod came down, the viewers couldn't see us. Celeste and I implied that her happiness led to us knocking down the curtain and causing Davey to nearly fall down in the tub. We all laughed at this plot development.

As the bathroom scene faded out, the next shot faded in with a slowly zooming-in exterior shot of Robert and Caroline's home. It was the same home that viewers would remember seeing in our old show. Of course, the image had been altered to suggest that this wasn't the 1980s or 1990s. The next scene faded in with the classic living room set from the old show with some modern updates. To suggest that the series was a dream, some items were changed to reflect that. The camera turned and zoomed onto the front door. This resembled the old front door from the series. However, it was implied that the front door had been replaced. The door had a peephole and the house address numbers tacked on. These elements would become crucial near the end of the movie.

In the next scene, two shadows passed a window to the left of the front door. It was Celeste and me. In this scene,

Debbie wanted to visit Davey's parents' home, to see if all was fine. Celeste and I improvised some dialogue that suggested as a married couple, why they were there. The studio camera followed as I unlocked the door and we walked in.

"You said that your parents were away on a cruise for the next two weeks," declared Celeste.

"That's right," I answered. "They wanted Robin to look after the place while they were gone. They were unsure what our schedules would be like, and we told them we planned to take a vacation next week."

"I wanted to come over to make sure all was like it should be."

As I closed the door, I said, "As you can see so far, nothing has changed since we were over the other day."

Celeste made her way toward the stairway. Then, she noticed the freestanding pictures on a nearby table. The camera followed her. The scene changed showing Celeste examining the photos. The first photo was Celeste and me. Two male child actors played our sons on the show. In the photo, we had taken a special picture to suggest this was Davey and Debbie's family picture. Celeste reached for another one. This one was of Kyle and Staci portraying Bryan and Robin. One male child actor and two female child actors had played the parts of her children. Unfortunately, the series suggested that Bryan and Robin had three girls, not two girls and a boy. The young male child actor was credited as a cousin in the 'dream' part of the show. In this 'reality' part, he was actually Bryan and Robin's son.

Finally, Celeste made her way to the last photo. I had been told that many were unsure who they would see in this photo until it aired. This picture was of Robert and Caroline Goodwin, the parents. Everyone was expecting to see Harry Pynchon standing with Marian Deavers. The audience was surprised. An older Terrence Forrester and an older Marian

Deavers were in this photo. Fortunately, a crew member had saved the original copy of this photo. I was told that they were lucky to find a copy from the original photo set taken for the first new show's pilot before the drastic recast.

A moment later, the front-door doorknob started rattling. I was still standing near the front door. I had noted to lock the door when I entered because this particular next scene was another one no one saw coming.

"Someone trying to break in?" asked Celeste.

"Sounds like someone is trying to use a key," I answered concerned, "because I locked the door."

"See who it is."

I walked to the front door and looked through the peephole then stepped away and whispered to Celeste, "Looks like the neighbor who lives a few houses down. Mr. Lozano."

Mr. Lozano started knocking and pounding on the door.

"Mr. Lozano, is that you?" I asked.

"Yes! What are you doing in my home?!" yelled a familiar voice from behind the front door.

After I unlocked and opened the door, I was facing Mr. Lozano. I was told that people laughed so much over this scene. Some said they had to pause the action because folks holding watch parties were laughing so hard as they enjoyed the small ironic visual joke. Many thought that casting Harry Pynchon in the movie's "reality" part as a nearby neighbor was a much-deserved "Hit the road!" for him and the late Albert Jacobs. We even had his character named Harry—Harry Lozano.

I know that seems rather harsh. Staci and Celeste had tried to talk with Harry—between taping takes and lunch breaks—about religion and Christ, but he refused to listen. He wanted nothing to do with Christianity. Staci, Celeste, and I had put in our contract demands that the original family members would be restored to the show. That meant Harry would have to play another character when the idea was devised to make the whole *"Goodwin Circles Around Again"* series and much of the *"Goodwin Circle: Returning Home"* final movie a terrible nightmare for Debbie Whitman. Unfortunately, we were unable to get Terrence Forrester and Marian Deavers to reprise their roles for the final part of the movie. Fortunately, we were able to visit with Terrence, Marian, and their respective families outside our taping times for this last TV movie. I can assure you that Terrence and Marian were happy with the final results.

"No offense, Harry..." I began.

"It's Mr. Lozano to you!" scolded Harry.

"Okay, Mr. Lozano. You're at the wrong house. This is the Goodwin house."

"I can see the address up there on the door!" exclaimed Harry. "This is my house!"

I turned to the door where the house numbers were. On the door, it read 1960.

"Mr. Lozano, one of these numbers has had a screw come loose," I said. "This is 1990 Wayward Drive, not 1960. You're at least three houses down the street on this side."

"Come on!" growled Harry. "You must have a screw loose! This *is* my house!"

I stepped closer and acted like I was sniffing in the direction of Harry's face.

"Is that alcohol on your breath?" I asked Harry.

"No, it's aftershave!" yelled Harry.

"That's strange. I've never smelled an aftershave like that. What's it called?"

Harry yelled, "I don't remember!"

I suggested Harry's aftershave was several shots of a well-known alcoholic beverage.

"You've been driving again?"

"Listen, kid! I don't want any trouble!"

"You've been told a thousand times to not get soused! Now you've done it again…"

"Please, kid! Leave me alone!" as Harry ran away out of the camera shot.

"If I see you back at my door like this, I'm calling the cops!"

I looked down on the ground within the covered porch and entryway. I noticed a screw on the faux concrete. It resembled one that belonged in the door. I picked up the screw. I retrieved a little screwdriver tool from my pocket. I turned the six clockwise to make it a nine and secured it. When done, I walked back in the house and closed the front door, locking it. The scene switched back to inside.

"That Mr. Lozano," I lustered. "I can't understand why he seems to do that all of the time."

I walked closer to the stairway. Then, Celeste and I heard a sound like a door opened upstairs.

"Someone's up there," Celeste said.

Another familiar voice came from upstairs said, "Is someone down there?"

"It's just Davey and me," said Celeste.

"I'll be down in a moment," said the voice.

A moment later, Staci came down the stairs. She pretended to yawn.

"Robin, what are you doing here?" I asked.

"I came by to check on the house," answered Staci. "I felt tired. I decided to take a nap on my old bed. Why are both of you here?"

Celeste answered, "I had a nightmare last night."

Staci asked, "Nightmare?"

"Debbie thought I had left her," I said to Staci. "Mom had died. Dad looked like that Mr. Lozano from down the street. Everybody had chosen to let everything else go, including morals and decency."

"Debbie?!" Staci in a concerned and caring voice.

I admitted, "Dreams can be weird, and feel so real." I stared off for a moment and then shook my head and then continued, "What I'm saying is, Debbie had a bad dream last night. She wanted to see the house. She wanted to know all was right."

"Mom and Dad aren't expected home for another week," answered Staci. "The last text message I received from them was that they're having fun."

"Alive, well, and enjoying their retirement years," I assured Celeste.

"That's good to know." Celeste was relieved as she walked toward the couch. "I can't believe that it's been such a long time since we met each other. Seems like yesterday."

The scene faded to when Davey met Debbie for the first time. The entire dialogue was shown without the blooper. Our real kids enjoyed seeing that scene again. The scene faded back to the "present" day.

"So what now?" asked Celeste.

"Well, we need to get going." I looked at my watch. "The boys will be back home soon."

Staci admitted, "I need to get home as well. Bryan has the kids."

"You stay in touch, ok?" I asked.

"Of course," assured Staci. "I'm just around the corner from you."

"I know." I smiled. "The kids like to visit their cousins when they can."

"I agree." Staci smiled.

"I'm so glad that I met both of you when I did," shared Celeste. "A wonderful loving husband. A terrific and caring friend and sister-in-law."

"I'm so glad that we met as well," answered Staci.

"I wouldn't have this beautiful wife if Robin hadn't mentored her in scouting," I said.

"There'll be other times to visit," assured Staci.

"Are you staying, Robin?" I asked.

"No," said Staci, "everything is the way Mom and Dad left it."

"We'll be glad to help check on the house later this week," said Celeste.

"I'll let you know," said Staci.

I turned to Staci and gave her a hug and kiss on her forehead. Celeste gave Staci a hug.

"You take care," I said to Staci.

Celeste said, "You take care, too, Robin."

"And both of you as well," said Staci.

Staci checked her pocket. She had her keys. We made our way to the front door and exited. The camera showed the dead bolt latch. The room lights dimmed suggesting that the room had never had any lights turned on. The scene changed showing all three of us exiting the porch, and the camera zooming out following us from the porch. The scene faded. Then, a memorial announcement was made to the young Tennessee college student who had died of the alcohol-induced poisoning at a college fraternity party.

The next scene faded into a picture of the front of the house. The closing credits rolled. Our family clapped and cheered. Over the next five minutes, the credits slowly scrolled with good pictures from both series. The final image was both families and the grandparents. The three pictures on the screen were the same ones that Celeste had viewed on the table by the stairway. When the credits concluded, the SYZ Studios logo and music fanfare played. This was followed by the FibreTainment logo and music fanfare. Then, the screen went black. A moment later, the menu screen with all of the show choices displayed. Everyone in our family was pleased with the TV movie conclusion.

A couple of nights later, the kids stayed with my parents while Staci's family was in town. This gave Celeste and me some time to unwind and to be together. On that particular night, KSFD chose to rerun our last *"Goodwin Circle"* TV movie from 2004 after the 10:00 p.m. news. I set the DVR to record the movie. It was going to be late when it ended since this movie started at 10:35 p.m., after the local news.

While Celeste and I watched from our recliners, we both drifted off to sleep. I must have been drifting in and out of sleep because I somehow dreamed that I was doing the voice-over of the nightly sign-off for KSFD Fort Worth-Dallas. It seemed so real.

I dreamed reading all of the technical details as different title cards and videos appeared on the "screen." I have included in an appendix—at the end of this book—what I said. Then, an old 1970s National Anthem film played. Following the anthem, an old-style test pattern with circles appeared with a 400 hertz tone. The tone woke me. I looked at my watch. It was 2:42 a.m. KSFD had signed off. I looked at the TV. Color bars filled the screen with a black bar at the top. Within the black bar, computer-generated-like text appeared—KSFD DFW. After a few more seconds of the test pattern, there was a quick hiss followed by a blue screen.

"It's nearly 2:45 a.m." I nudged Celeste in her recliner. "We need to go to bed."

Celeste awoke slowly, as I told her again, we needed to go to bed. We got up, and turned off the TV. It was just a quiet night. We were thankful for our family and friends. Celeste and I said a prayer as we turned in. For the rest of the night, we had a peaceful sleep. Despite all of the things that had happened over the last few years, God was truly glorified in the end!

APPENDIX A

---◆------◆------◆---

List of Bible Passages Kyle Selected and Prepared to Share with Staci in Chapter 8

3 John 1:11
Ephesians 5:1
Matthew 6:24
Deuteronomy 28:1-68
Galatians 5:19-21
Romans 2:1-29
Ephesians 5:11
1 Corinthians 11:1
Luke 10:27
Exodus 20:1-26
Matthew 5:19
Deuteronomy 28:47-48
Galatians 6:7
Leviticus 26:1-46
John 14:15
1 Corinthians 6:12
Proverbs 25:26
1 Corinthians 10:23
2 Timothy 2:22
1 Timothy 6:10
Hebrews 13:5
Ephesians 4:27
James 1:5
James 1:20
Ephesians 6:1-4
1 Corinthians 15:33
Romans 12:1
Romans 1:26-27
Matthew 18:6
1 Corinthians 10:31

2 Timothy 3:16-17
2 Timothy 2:19
Ephesians 4:31-32
Colossians 3:1
https://www.openbible.info/topics/acting was the source for
the location of these verses.
Kyle explained to Staci about the Romans 14 passage that
our care pastor Justin had discussed with us. This was in
reference to the photo controversy that had happened on
Staci's social media pages months ago.
Kyle also mentioned:
Romans 12
Matthew 16:26
Mark 8:36
Luke 9:23-25
1 Corinthians 3:13
1 Timothy 6:10
Proverbs 6:23-33
Matthew 5:17-20
Matthew 5:27-30
Proverbs 7:4-9
Romans 13:8-14
Philippians 2:1-18 with emphasis on Philippians 2:3,
Philippians 2:9-11, and Philippians 2:14-16
James 4:7
Isaiah 40:8
2 Corinthians 5:21
Psalms 101:3
Titus 2:7-8
1 John 1:9
1 John 2:15
Philippians 4:8-9
Psalms 101:3
and once again, 1 Corinthians 10:31

APPENDIX B

———◆———◆———◆———

Mike's Dream – Script for the Sign Off

Mike dreamed reading the following:

"At this time, KSFD, Fort Worth-Dallas concludes another broadcast day in the public interest of beautiful north Texas.

KSFD is owned by The American SuperChannel Stations of Texas, LLC, a subsidiary of the ASC Television Network, and operated by the ASC Television Stations Division.

KSFD operates its studios at 1 Superchannel Drive in Fort Worth and 3129 Gerald Knobele Drive in Dallas. We also operate news bureaus in Sherman, Denton, Terrell, and Weatherford.

Operating with circular polarization and a maximum effective radiated power of five-million watts, KSFD broadcasts from our transmitter in Cedar Hill, Texas— at a height of 1,990 feet—by authority of the Federal Communications Commission.

KSFD is a member in good standing of the Texas Association of Broadcasters and the National Association of Broadcasters. We proudly display this Seal of Good Practice as a subscriber to the NAB Television Code. For the best in television viewing, tune to KSFD, a TV Code station.

KSFD welcomes your questions, comments, and concerns. Please send them to KSFD-TV, General Manager, 3129 Gerald Knobele Drive, Dallas, TX.

Portions of the preceding day's broadcast were mechanically reproduced on film, slides, and videotape.

We thank you for joining us today, and we hope that you will join us again later this morning at five o'clock for another broadcast day.

Until then, speaking on behalf of the management and staff of KSFD Fort Worth-Dallas, 'The Great SuperChannel of the Southwest' we wish you a pleasant good night and good morning. Ladies and gentlemen, our National Anthem."

An old film with the "Star Spangled Banner—National Anthem" played next.

ABOUT THE AUTHOR

John R. Price is a Christian, loving husband, college teacher, and writer in the greater Little Rock, Arkansas Metro area. For over 40 years, he has loved watching classic television and following the entertainment industry as a hobby. He also enjoys studying Christian apologetics.

He is married to his lovely wife, Anna.